STALLION'S INSTINCT

A DAY CARE FOR SHIFTERS
BOOK FIVE

ELVA BIRCH

A WORLD OF INSTINCT

Bearing North *is set in the larger* ***World of Instinct***, *a setting with secret shifters, elementals, and magical instinct.*

A Day Care for Shifters is a swoony, sweet-hot series set in the small town of Nickel City, where shifters are trying to stay secret…something infinitely complicated by young shifters just learning their magical skills, right along with walking and talking and stealing hearts! These are gentle romances full of humor and feeling, perfect ice-cream-straight-from-the-container escapes that each stand alone.

Wolf's Instinct: Roderick's toddler daughter and busy plumbing business keep him too wrapped up for romance and while he trusts his wolf, the magic of instinct can be like playing hot-and-cold with a kid who's forgotten where they hid the prize. Addison comes to Nickel City to take a job at a very special day care and finds a family to belong to.

First Comes Love (a mini-series!): Navigating on-line dating is hard enough for a single mom and first shift baker, but Chloe has a whole new set of problems when her little boy suddenly changes into a pushy baby penguin and Clay, a polar bear shifter comes to her rescue. This mini-trilogy includes three short stories: First Shift, First Day, and First Date, all collected with two more bonus stories in First Comes Love, with adorable illustrations by Ellen Million!

Dragon's Instinct: Ian had enough trouble trying to write for a living and keep up with his daughter, Lucy, even before she started shifting into a squirrel. Now that she's turning two and breathing fire? The twos just got a lot more terrible!

Unicorn's Instinct: Tara just wants her mommy to be happy…and a puppy. Vivian doesn't have the heart or time for romance, let alone a puppy, but everything changes when she meets the new pediatric doctor at her clinic and learns his heart-breaking secret.

Gryphon's Instinct: Theo is a single dad chasing two kids—including a teleporting baby gryphon!—and Wendy is just weird enough to fit their family perfectly.

Bearly Better Yeti: *She's looking for a monster…and finds a mate!* Polar bear shifter Oliver got caught on camera at the worst possible time and now Molly Flash, a cryptid-hunting internet celebrity, is snooping around the lake looking for a yeti. A novella at Belle Lake Lodge.

Stallion's Instinct: He's a playboy, cowboy, and con man, suddenly saddled with a four-year-old filly shifter!

Raven's Instinct: Ravens like shiny things…(coming in 2025)

You can also get signed and sketched paperbacks at my webpage: elvabirch.com!

1

*L*ogan hated cheap stock trailers, whether he was a horse or a man.

They were loud and hollow-sounding, and being dragged in one for miles down dusty gravel roads was a special kind of torture. When Logan was a horse, there was no way to move around or turn; it was painfully dull and boring. When he was a man, there were no concessions for his form (it was too suspicious to have human comforts in a box made for livestock), so he rattled around in a hot, empty tin can. If he sat down on the floor to use his phone, he had no view, and if he stood up to look out, he had to cling to the side or stagger at every curve, with only two legs to balance on.

Either way was uncomfortable and irritating.

"Next time, *you're* the horse," he groused at Clancy when they arrived at the Montana ranch, after he'd confirmed that the trailer was angled so it wasn't visible from the farmhouse and there was no one in sight yet.

"You're the more valuable specimen," his cousin reminded him out as he put out the ramp. His voice got silky. "Who's a pretty boy with fake papers? Now shift, because the nice lady with the deep pockets is coming."

Logan's instinct gave an unhelpful warble. Something was off about this deal, but Logan couldn't tell what, so he stuffed his misgivings down without examining their cause. Instinct was like a fortune cookie anyway, right just often enough to be frustrating, and annoyingly vague. Deals with Clancy always left him feeling dirty, and it was no different ignoring magical instinct than it was to ignore his remorse.

Grumbling, he shifted and high-stepped out of the trailer. *Let's go put on a goddamn show.*

His stallion, to Logan's disgust, was happy to toss his mane and let the long, coarse hair spill down over his arched neck. *We **should** be admired. We are amazing. Look how beautiful the light on us is!*

Humility was not one of his animal's stronger traits.

"Dammit, Logan, you aren't wearing a halter!" Clancy hissed.

Logan could take simple items with him and back from form to form, and he cursed himself for such a stupid over-sight; he must not have been wearing one the last time he'd been a horse. Well, if anyone could pull off trying to sell a horse with no halter, it would be Clancy, who was as smooth-talking as any car or snake oil salesman.

"You must be Jason Commingson. Nice to meet you. My vet will be here shortly."

Logan wheeled to face their customer. Tabby Swiftwater was a tall woman, strong and curvy, with arms that showed muscle. She wore jeans with pale knees and a faded T-shirt, a brimmed cowboy hat shading her eyes from the morning sun. Her gaze was sharp and unwavering. Everything about her suggested a woman who was used to working hard and Logan had to keep himself from crowding possessively as his cousin stepped forward to shake her hand with an appreciative grin. He didn't want to come across as an aggressive animal and scare the buyer off before they even began.

Logan found himself wishing they were here for any reason other than a horse sale. Tabby was exactly the kind of woman he'd want to buy a drink for at a bar, with a blue-collar beauty that deeply appealed to him.

"Should he be out without a halter on?" she asked, giving Clancy's hand a brisk shake but looking only at Logan. Disapproval was obvious in her voice.

"He's trained up a treat, ma'am," Clancy explained without hesitation. "Just as described. He's a Dutch warmblood, seventeen hands of muscle and manners that will jump over anything that stands still long enough. Did you have a chance to review the papers I sent?"

Logan pranced delicately in place and lowered his head to blow gently at Tabby. She smelled delicious, like sun and dry grass and faintly of sweat, and Logan had to keep himself from lipping her eagerly when she extended her hand.

"Oh, he's a beauty," she said, melting and stroking his nose. "Of course I looked over the papers. It's an *impressive* lineage." The glance she gave Clancy suggested that she recognized how dubious his claims were, but she didn't challenge them.

"He'd throw some prize foals if you're looking to set up a breeding stock," Clancy said coaxingly.

Logan wished he was an ostrich shifter so he could bury his face in the sand. Here was the woman of his dreams, and he was a fifteen hundred pound piece of meat.

*We **would** make beautiful foals*, his stallion said proudly.

No. The answer is no. Not ever.

You could sire them on this woman, his stallion suggested. *She looks fertile and strong.*

She's a person, Logan insisted. *She's not a means to a legacy and neither am I.*

We should have a herd, his stallion complained.

We have a cousin and a brother. Logan was not close with his immediate family, except for Clancy…and there wasn't as much affection between the two of them as there was grudging loyalty. They needed each other for their marketing strategy, but Logan didn't trust Clancy beyond those bonds, and his stallion didn't consider him *herd.* Logan hadn't talked to his brother, Steven, in five years.

We should have a mare and foals of our own to protect, his horse insisted, single-minded and mule-headed.

This is not a conversation I am having, Logan said firmly. Kids were not part of his equation, not ever.

He was a con man, not a family man, and this arrangement had suited them just fine.

Until now.

Until Tabby Swiftwater waltzed into the picture with her battered boots and deep brown eyes.

Because this woman didn't have only his stallion's attention, but all of Logan's as well. He'd never seen someone so sexy, and besides that, she seemed charming and clever, and Logan felt like he'd just been caught in a flytrap of irrational affection.

Tabby was frowning now, and shaking her head earnestly.

"I'm not as interested in breed as I am in work ethic. I want a strong jumper and I don't have a setup for a stallion. I'm trying to start a school, not a dynasty." She was still stroking Logan's nose, like she couldn't resist.

"You can always have him gelded," Clancy observed.

GELDED? his stallion protested.

Logan could feel any ardor shriveling and he stepped straight sideways into Clancy.

"Oof, he's got a sense of humor, this one," Clancy wheezed, barely keeping his balance. "But I promise, he's *sweet as can be.*" He bumped Logan back with his shoulder, but it was hardly an equal hit. "Let me put him through his paces, and you'll see for yourself."

"You don't have a saddle or a lead," Tabby pointed out skeptically, drawing back.

"This baby doesn't need one," Clancy said confidently. "He's been free lunging since he was a baby. Step out, Better Behave."

Logan put his ears back. Clancy delighted in giving him ridiculous names. It was in keeping with equine tradition, and it wasn't the worst name he'd been stuck with.

"Does he have a barn name?" Tabby wanted to know.

"You can call him anything you want, honey," Clancy said expansively.

Logan wished he was making a better impression on Tabby. He was torn between desperation to awe her and thinking about deliberately muffing his routine so that Clancy couldn't close the deal. He wasn't sure what instinct, humming in his head like angry bees, was trying to tell him, but he was positive that he didn't want to start things out with Tabby by taking all her money.

The thought arrested him.

What could he possibly be *starting out* with Tabby?

When he paused to examine this startling idea, his stallion took advantage of his hesitation and took off without Logan's conscious control, lifting his feet and dancing forward into a pitch-perfect canter for the far gate.

"Trot, you aptly named asshole!" Clancy hollered after him.

Logan did a brief, springy circuit of the pen.

"He's gorgeous," Tabby whispered. "That *gait*."

There were jumps set up, homebuilt from painted dimension lumber, and Logan sprang over each of them on his way back, clearing with distance to spare and landing lightly before he circled back to where Clancy and Tabby were watching. He ended in a high-stepping prance and stopped on a dime. Tabby didn't flinch at his approach, but stood her ground and gazed up at him with smitten eyes.

"He's a desperate showoff," Clancy said with an apologetic laugh. "Smug bastard," he added below his breath.

Logan stood contritely before them at complete attention. Tabby touched him again, stroking his neck, and his whole hide seemed to go electric. Logan had been affected by a pretty face and hot body before, but nothing at such a bone-deep level.

"He's a beauty," Tabby agreed helplessly.

Don't buy me, Logan thought as hard as he could, wishing that telepathy came with shifting. *Don't break your heart on a jerk like me.*

"He's a steal at this price," Clancy said, and Logan marveled at the sincerity in his voice. "But I want him to go to a home that will love him. I wouldn't be selling him at all if I didn't have my mother's cancer to cover."

Too thick, Logan thought ferociously at his cousin. *Don't do this to her.*

But Clancy couldn't hear him any more than Tabby could.

"I'll need to see him under a rider," Tabby said practically. "And my vet will be here shortly to check him out. You should discount your price for the fact that I'll have to pay for the gelding."

GELDING? His stallion snorted and stepped back in

affront before Logan could stop him to maintain their cover.

We'll be gone before she has a chance to do that, Logan reminded him.

Instinct gave a twang that felt like regret, and Logan squashed it down. This was only business.

2

———————

*T*abby wondered if she was making a terrible mistake. Buying this horse would clean out her savings account, but she was confident that *this* was the horse that could set her dreams in motion.

She'd never seen an animal like Better Behave. Terrible name aside, he was tall, springy, smart, and motivated. His gaits were perfect, his manners impeccable. A swirl of blowing leaves that might have spooked a high-strung mount was completely ignored.

Clancy rode him around the ring without a saddle to prove that he wasn't going to become mysteriously lame under the weight of a rider. The vet took x-rays in his mobile shop and declared him sound, quietly admitting to Tabby that he was a prize for the price.

Better Behave jumped like a rabbit, strutted like a dressage horse, cornered like a rodeo barrel-racer, and Tabby guessed that he could pull like a Budweiser Clydesdale. His calmness suggested he'd be a good trail horse once he retired from jumping.

He was gorgeous, a deep bay with a curious white

streak in his forelock. There were no other white markings and Tabby wondered if it was a throwback to some ancestor that didn't show in his papers (which were probably forged), an old injury, or just an odd genetic fluke.

His attention to Tabby was almost uncanny, and Tabby wasn't too proud to admit that she fell utterly in love with him at first sight.

Love was an awful basis for a business decision, and she could hear her mother tsking a warning in her ear. *You have terrible judgment,* her mother's ghost reminded her. *You've lost your shirt before by trusting pretty men.*

But Jason Commingson wasn't particularly pretty, and Tabby didn't trust him an inch. She was one hundred percent positive the dying mother was fictional and knew that papers could be faked, but she wasn't interested in pedigree, only in performance, and Better Behave was so gorgeous and graceful that she was completely willing to do business with a snake oil salesman to get him.

It almost looked like the two were tussling when she returned to the yard with a pen to sign the papers, like the big horse was trying to herd the man back into the shabby stock trailer and "Jason" was arguing with him out loud.

"Would you relax? You know how this goes. It's fine. You'll keep your nuts. She's coming right back, knock it off, you buffoon."

Better Behave—she was going to have to find something better to call him—gave a snort and stomped one hoof in the dirt, narrowly missing Jason's foot as the man looked up with an expression of dismay.

"Oh, Miss Swiftwater. Let's make this official." Jason took the pen and retreated to the cab of the truck.

That left Tabby alone with the horse and he gave a tired sigh of defeat and hung his head.

Tabby could not resist touching him, stroking his silky

hide and feeling the smooth, strong muscles under his flawless skin. "You're a beauty," she murmured. He really was. He was a shining dark mahogany brown, broken only by that brilliant half-white forelock.

"Here we go," Jason said. He gave her the papers and waited expectantly.

Tabby looked through the papers as carefully as she could, verifying that it hadn't been altered from the version she'd seen earlier, then took a deep breath, signed them and pulled out her phone. It was the largest wire she'd ever sent.

Jason's face was suspiciously bland. "Call me in the next few days if anything comes up, but I'm confident that you'll be *wildly* happy with this *fine* stallion."

Better Behave gave a snort that was almost a laugh as Jason tipped his cowboy hat at Tabby and took his copies of the contract. The horse sidled back from the truck and trailer even before it was started up.

Tabby wasn't sorry to see the man leave and gave a sigh of relief.

She'd gotten her horse.

"Let's go get you fitted with some tack," Tabby said, guiding him with a simple hand at his neck. "I cannot wait to have you between my legs."

Better Behave tripped on nothing and caught himself immediately.

It was the first time she'd seen the elegant animal stumble, and for a moment, Tabby was afraid that she really had been fleeced. Then he snorted and shook his head, following her willingly to the barn without further hesitation.

Tabby had a close-contact saddle big enough to span the horse's broad back, and he stood patiently while Tabby settled it on and tightened the girth. He didn't attempt any tricks to make it loose or try to sidle away. He took the bit and bridle with an almost human eye roll, and then Tabby was leading him to the mounting block and stepping into the stirrup to swing herself over with the reins in her hand.

He moved out at the tiniest squeeze of her calves, flowing into an impulsive gallop for the far side of the field.

"Whoa!" Tabby called, tugging at the reins and sitting back in the saddle. His cool conduct hadn't prepared her for outright disobedience, and she began to wonder if his name was more appropriate than she realized. He circled and lined up for the jumps, and Tabby gave him his head, settling herself in the saddle as he stretched out for the obstacles.

It was like riding on a thunderstorm or a tidal wave. He was power and precision, and he was mathematically perfect with every step. Seeing him jump in the videos that Jason sent had been one thing. Watching him in person was a second level of joy. But riding him?

His takeoffs were smooth and his landings were flaw-less. It was like flying, or being struck by lightning. It was everything she'd ever dreamed of, with a partner under her who intuitively understood exactly what she wanted of him, and delivered it with flair she'd never imagined.

He circled to take them again, and Tabby turned him towards the gate, instead. She'd spent most of her day buying him already, but she could indulge in a short trail ride before she got back to her other work, and there was nowhere she wanted to be more than on his back. They deserved a victory lap.

He stood stock still while she bent to release the gate latch, and when they were through, he backed up so that she could secure it again behind them like he knew how the mechanism worked. It must have been something he'd been trained to do with his previous rider. He didn't get worked up as they passed the barn, though as a stallion, he must have scented the mares inside. His manners were *irreproachable.*

And he was a joy to ride, with a smooth, light-footed gait down the trail. He didn't shy at the rustling autumn leaves or sighing grasses, and he launched over the little creek and downed trees with delight. It was midmorning and the sun had burnt off the frost in open places, but it still sparkled in the forest shade. Tabby couldn't resist a quick canter when the path was good, but she'd test a longer gallop when they had more time and space. She turned them reluctantly back to the ranch at the first branch in the trail. He huffed in disappointment, as if he knew it would circle them back, then went willingly.

If he had been the tiniest bit less well-trained, he'd be a disaster, with his independence and strength. Instead, he was gentle and clever. He was everything she'd ever hoped for in a horse.

Was it cheating to ride him in competitions, when he was so absolutely perfect out of the box? It wouldn't be a true testament to her training skills. But now that she'd ridden him, Tabby could not imagine a better mount.

Tabby got him a fresh net of hay at the barn, topped off his water, then shut his stall door firmly and set the security system at the outer stable door as she left. Maybe she was being unreasonably suspicious of Jason; she'd paid a fair price for a great horse, and if he embellished his story a little, well, selling horses came with a certain amount of theatrics at the best of times.

Tabby rushed through dinner and other duties, attended to her boarders, and lingered over Better Behave. "You don't deserve that name," she told him, brushing him unnecessarily. "You need a magnificent name. Something regal. King? Duke? Not Duke. And I won't name you after a food. Maybe Beau. You're a heartthrob, for sure."

Out of fairness, she gave the other horses a little extra attention, too, then dragged herself to bed feeling triumphant and optimistic.

The next morning, her first sign that something was wrong was that the security pad at the barn was greenlit. The door slid open without requiring the code and Tabby bolted in to find that Better Behave was gone.

Tabby checked every stall, as if she might have forgotten which one he had been in, and verified that every one of them was still latched tight. Trudy, Oreo, and Angus were all placidly in place, so it hadn't been a general heist. Tabby went back to Better Behave's stall. She'd had clever horses before, and knew how to keep a stable secure. The door was solid, with bars above that a horse couldn't fit its nose through even if he could wrangle a simple latch.

He was simply *gone.*

The stall was secured from the outside. Nothing was broken. There was *no way* that he could have gotten out of his stall and latched it behind him again without human hands. And the barn security system had been disarmed from the *inside.* Even if Better Behave had been the smartest horse in the history of the universe, the keypad required fingers.

Tabby sank down on the bench outside the barn.

She'd spent all of her money on a horse, and her greatest grief was not losing her shirt, but losing that gorgeous animal. She didn't consider herself a sentimental person, and she certainly didn't believe in fairy tales, but she'd utterly lost her heart at the first sight of that horse, and now she'd *lost* him.

A few hot tears slipped down her cheeks. She worked hard and tried to be a good person. She paid her taxes and only sped a little when the roads were safe. She treated people well and tipped generously. It wasn't *fair* that this had happened to her. It wasn't fair to have all her hope snatched away from her *again*.

Tabby only allowed herself a moment of self-pity before climbing to her feet and wiping her face. She wasn't going to let this stop her. She was going to find that sonuvabitch if it took her last pennies, and she was going to get her horse back.

3

SIX MONTHS LATER

"You were a hard man to track down, Mr. Kennedy. Did you know that we've been looking for you for nearly two years?"

Logan stared hard at the woman, trying to figure out how to politely explain that he didn't want to be found. She had tired, patient eyes as she sat behind her cluttered desk. She gestured to a seat that Logan didn't take.

"Look, this is a terrible mistake, Mrs. Gravis." He shouldn't have taken the call in the first place. He should have burned the phone that social services had called him on and changed his identity again.

He couldn't remember how the case worker had talked him into coming, let alone agreeing to meet his brother's daughter, and the drive had given him plenty of time to regret making the promise. "You said that she was with a foster family. She should stay with them. I'm no kind of dad. I didn't even know that Steven had died, or that he had a daughter."

Logan suspected that Mrs. Gravis had gone through this conversation before, because she didn't seem surprised.

"A lot of people think that, Mr. Kennedy, but it's almost always for the best to place a child with their family. We're here to offer any support that you need."

"Doesn't she already have that support?" Logan asked desperately. "Isn't it better not to uproot her and just leave her where she is? How could it possibly be better to give her to an uncle she doesn't even know?"

Mrs. Gravis stood, and her eyes looked even more tired and patient as she rounded the desk. "We have a lot of kids in the foster system that need her space. Our budget is not infinite, and many of our foster homes are only temporary. Franzi's already been in several homes, and she needs stability, Mr. Kennedy."

"Logan," he corrected.

But it was worse when she called him that. "Logan, it's a miracle that we found you, and I know in my heart that you are the best possible guardian for your brother's little girl."

"What if I refuse?" Logan asked stubbornly. "I only agreed to meet her. I haven't signed anything."

"If you won't take her, we've also recently found contact information for her next nearest blood relative, Clancy Kennedy."

"No!" Logan answered before his brain had even caught up with him. He'd severed his relationship with Clancy six months earlier, wracked with guilt about fleecing Tabby Swiftwater. Conning arena owners and speculative billionaires was one thing, but Logan couldn't stomach the guilt of taking the life savings of someone whose only flaw was being gullible.

Their quarrel had escalated to a complete falling out, and Clancy had cut Logan out of his racket altogether.

Had he found another horse shifter to do shell games with? Or someone to sell him? As a mixed blood pony, Clancy didn't have the same sales value as Logan, but there was still money to be made as a human-smart horse, and live-stock sales weren't Clancy's only swindle. There was no way Clancy had gone straight, or that he ever would, even if he got saddled with a little kid.

"No," Logan said again. "Not Clancy."

There was a little glint of triumph in the case worker's eyes. "Let's go meet Frances."

Feeling like he'd just been taken for a ride, Logan reluc-tantly followed her out of the office and down the hall.

*Logan's first impression of Frances Kennedy was that she was much tinier than he was expecting.

She was barely larger than a doll, sitting on the edge of a couch with her legs hanging over. She wore a pair of pink overalls over a white shirt with short puffed sleeves, both of them slightly stained, and held a small plastic pitcher. The playroom was filled with well-used toys. A dated plastic kitchen overflowing with plastic food and mismatched dishes stood in one corner, and cluttered shelves of kids books ran under the windows. A miniature metal shopping cart missing one wheel listed to its side, filled with taped-shut cereal boxes and empty milk cartons.

The girl looked up hopefully at their entrance, dark hair bouncing in loose curls around blue eyes, but she waited in place rather than running to greet them.

Little filly! Logan's stallion said, nearly swooning.

Even from here, Logan could tell that she was a shifter, though there was no way of knowing if she was a horse. Probably she was, because Steven had been, and their father, as well. Magical instinct gave that particular little shiver of recognition that every shifter got when they met another of their kind, but it wasn't specific. Most kids began shifting at the age of two, which was right when her dad had died. Had the loss stunted her ability? Had she been able to keep her power a secret, or had this complicated her placement with foster families?

Logan eyed Mrs. Gravis cautiously, unsure of how much to say or what to ask. He could tell that the case worker wasn't a shifter, and shifting was secret, for good reason. He couldn't just come out and ask, 'Oh, by the way, has she turned into a horse recently?'

"This is your uncle Logan," Mrs. Gravis introduced cheerfully. "Do you want to come say hi, Frances?"

Frances ducked her head and pulled her feet up underneath her on the couch.

"You don't have to," Logan said, coming slowly into the room. He kept his voice low and gentle. He might not know about kids, but he knew how to handle sketchy horses and shy animals. "I'm happy to meet you, Frances."

She seemed to relax a notch at that.

"Your uncle is going to take you home with him," the case worker said confidently, avoiding Logan's quick glance. He'd promised nothing of the sort, but he didn't want to argue about it in front of Frances.

Did Frances's shoulders sag in disappointment? Did she want to stay with the last family she'd been with? Steven had been dead for two years, how many foster families had she been through?

"Franzi," she mumbled.

"What?"

She repeated the word again, even softer.

"Is Franzi your name?" Logan asked, coming closer to

hear and squatting down so he wouldn't be so tall and frightening.

She stared at him with big, sorrowful eyes and nodded.

"I'll call you Franzi," Logan promised. "That's a pretty name."

That won him a ghost of a smile.

How did you converse with a four-year-old? Should he mention her father and talk about when they were boys? Did she even remember Steven? "I like your pitcher," he said desperately.

"It's a TEApot," Franzi insisted. "For TEA."

"Of course," Logan agreed.

"I make tea!" Franzi slid fearlessly off the couch and dashed to the play kitchen, where she rattled things around rather alarmingly, opening and shutting cabinet doors. There was a fake microwave that gave a tired little chime when it was opened and closed, and that seemed to be a very necessary thing to do over and over.

Franzi kept up a string of chatter as she worked, but Logan could honestly not pick a single sentence out of it.

"I'll go get the papers together," Mrs. Gravis said, patting his shoulder.

Logan didn't stop her, but sank down to sit cross-legged on the floor as he watched Franzi and wondered what he had gotten himself into.

She was definitely older than a toddler, but not quite a kindergartener, Logan guessed. He knew that she was four, but didn't really understand what being four meant. Was she potty trained? Could she feed herself? Would she roll off a bed? Did Logan need a crib for her?

"I've got a place in Billings." Logan wished he hadn't left it quite such a mess. "Would you like to come see it and decide if you'd like to live there?"

Franzi stared at him so long that he started to wonder

how much she'd actually understood. Then she jerked her chin down in a decisive nod and handed an empty plastic cup to Logan. "It's HOT," she warned.

Logan pretended to sip and handed it back.

"Drink more!" Franzi commanded, and she wouldn't take the cup until Logan fake-drank at least a gallon out of the two-ounce vessel. "All gone!" she announced, and she took the cup. "I make more!"

Mrs. Gravis came back while Franzi made the microwave beep at least a hundred times making a new cup of tea.

Logan signed the papers in a daze, and took possession of two old suitcases. "This is all she has?"

"She's lucky to have suitcases," Mrs. Gravis said tartly. "A lot of our kids have to transport their things in garbage bags, and can you imagine how that feels?"

"She must have had clothes from Steven…" Logan realized as he spoke that it had been two years since Franzi had a father, and she must have grown in that time. Did she even *remember* Steven?

"Do you have a car seat, Mr. Kennedy?"

Logan stared at her in horror. "I didn't even think of that. I should have thought of that."

"It's okay, Mr. Kennedy. We have some loaners here that I can check out to you. We'll send someone out to your house in a few days to make sure you have a safe envi- ronment for her, and if there's anything you need, we have some start-up supplies for you. Do you need food?"

"Play food," Logan blurted. "She seems to like the plastic stuff in the pretend kitchen, and I don't have anything like that."

"We get lots of that donated," Mrs. Gravis said kindly. "I'll find you a box."

"Yes," Logan said faintly. "That would be great."

~

*L*ogan hefted the car seat up into the passenger seat and strapped it into place, following the tiny, nearly indecipherable instructions on the side. By the time he had stumbled through the steps for cinching and leveling, he was alarmed to find that Frances wasn't at the side of the truck where he'd left her. He startled away from the truck in a blind panic to find her wandering out into the parking lot. "Wait, Frances! Franzi! You can't go out there! Come back, *right now!*"

For a terrible moment, Logan was afraid that she would defy him and run away because he'd yelled, and he wondered how it would look to have to chase her down and whether she would scream and cry and kick.

"Okay," she said mildly, trotting back. She seemed perfectly happy to have him lift her up and Logan was struck by how light she was. How could there be so much person in such a fragile package?

And how could she mean so much already?

Her arms clutched around his neck and for one brief moment, she rested her cheek against his. Logan felt like he'd lost his heart.

Our filly! his stallion sang. *Our herd!* Then, because he was insufferable, he had to add, *I told you so.*

Shut up, you glue factory reject, Logan retorted, setting Franzi carefully into the car seat and trying to figure out where all the limbs and straps went. It was more complicated than a race car harness. Fortunately, Franzi knew how to sort herself out, although she didn't have the hand strength to actually attach the buckle.

Conversing with a four-year-old proved to be exhausting.

Logan could only understand about half of what she

said as they made the three hour drive. Some words she articulated perfectly and some seemed to be complete nonsense. She merrily babbled about things they drove past and played pretend games of "I'm a princess!" and "I'm a"—probably not a roadmap or a kettle of liver.

Logan might not be able to ask Mrs. Gravis about shifting, but he could ask Franzi. "Honey, are you…are you a horsey?"

It was the first thing that completely silenced her since they'd left social services and Logan risked taking his eyes off the road to look at her.

"Not SUPOZE to be a horsey," Franzi said stiffly, staring at her hands.

Maybe Steven had trained it into her to keep it a secret. Logan didn't want to risk disrupting what little trust they had developed, so he dropped the subject. "Look, there's a cow!"

Franzi craned her head to see, and after a few more miles, she was back to chattering.

Logan slowly realized he didn't have to understand everything and stopped asking her to repeat things. All he had to do was nod, agree, and laugh when she seemed to think something should be funny, letting her words drone into background noise as he wondered again what on earth he'd gotten into.

He didn't notice at first when she went silent, and then he glanced over and found that she'd fallen asleep sitting upright, her head tilted back and her mouth slightly open.

The final miles to his shabby apartment were strangely lonely.

Logan unpacked the truck while she continued to sleep, and after staring at her in consternation for a moment, he finally unbuckled her and got her out of the car seat without waking her.

She snuggled against him with a sigh and Logan felt his heart give a little twang.

Shut up, he told his stallion preemptively.

I didn't say anything, he snorted back. *But I told you so.*

Logan's bed was a wreck, so he settled Franzi on the couch and found a blanket to drape over her.

He was fussing unnecessarily, tucking in the corners, when there was a loud knock. Maybe one of his unsavory neighbors had seen him come in and was being nosy. Logan went to the door and yanked it open, planning to ask them to keep it down.

Instead, he stared, the words dying on his lips.

Tabby Swiftwater was standing in the apartment hall with her hands on her hips, as irresistible as ever. "I'm looking for Clancy Kennedy," she said furiously. "He sold me a stolen horse."

4

The man who answered the door was not Clancy Kennedy, otherwise known as Jason Commingson.

He was taller, broader, and far better-looking. He was wearing a cowboy hat and a Western shirt that was unbuttoned one button too far, making him look like a stripper who was pretending to be a cowboy. Tabby would have put money on the fact that he'd never mucked a stall or been on a horse that wasn't paid for with a quarter.

He also looked like he'd just caught a hurricane in a bottle and wasn't sure what to do with it. He couldn't quite hide his look of alarm when he heard Clancy's real name, so Tabby knew she was close to her quarry, and she refused to be sidetracked by a handsome cowpoke Magic Mike.

"Where is he?" she demanded.

He glanced behind him, but it wasn't a guilty look. "Keep it down," he hissed. "She's sleeping."

There was a little girl curled on the couch, wrapped in a cheap quilt. She had brown curls over an angelic face, slack with sleep. Little fists clutched at the blanket; she couldn't have been more than four.

The house, aside from the sleeping child, looked like a bachelor crash-pad. Some attempt had clearly been made to clean it, and there was a box of toys on top of the kitchen table, but there was a motorcycle in parts taking up most of the living room, and the art and decor suggested *single guy clinging to his youth*. The only artwork was posters of beer ads and half-dressed women. They were tacked to the wall, not even framed.

"Clancy Kennedy," Tabby said firmly. "Where is he?"

"I don't know," the man said, and he looked too frazzled to be lying as he pulled off his hat and dragged his fingers through dark hair in need of a cut. He had a curious shock of bright white hair that suggested he was older than he otherwise looked. "I honestly have no idea, and I'd be happy not to ever see him again. Look, I'm really sorry about…whatever he did to you, but I can't help you. *I can't help you.*"

Tabby didn't offer to go, and he didn't offer to close the door on her. They stood in a standoff until even Tabby could recognize that it was awkward. "You're his cousin, right? Logan Kennedy?"

"We're not close," Logan said defensively.

"Well, do you know someone who *would* know where he was?" Tabby asked impatiently. She was not going to let this be another dead end. "Under any of his many, many names? Jason Commingson? Harvey Killroy, maybe?"

That earned her a look of surprise. "How'd you figure that out?"

"I'm a smart cookie," Tabby snapped. "And Clancy isn't as clever as he thinks he is."

Logan gave a loud snort of laughter and turned in alarm to make sure it hadn't woken the little girl. She slumbered on, in that limp, lost way that only the truly young are capable of.

"Child services said they know where he is," Logan said thoughtfully. "But I know Clancy. He won't have any of your money left."

"I don't want his money. I want the horse he sold me. That he's sold a dozen times, apparently, across seven different states, now. Is that his kid?" Tabby wasn't sure that she was desperate enough to leverage his child against the guy who had cheated him, but she *was* pretty desperate.

"No, it's—she's *mine* now. My brother's. He's dead. I'm all she's got. Her name is Franzi."

"Oh." Tabby felt her resolve crumble before pity. "Oh, I'm so sorry."

"We weren't close," Logan said, but he said it regretfully. "For a lot of reasons, and Clancy was one of them. Do you know anything about kids? I have to get the house childproofed before social service's visit and I don't even know what that means. I mean, I tried to leave their office without a car seat. They just handed me a *kid*. I have no idea what I'm doing."

He was gorgeous, but he had a wild look around his eyes, and if Tabby hadn't been sorry for him before, she definitely was now.

"I usually deal with older kids," she admitted. "But let's start with the biggest risks. Do you have any guns?"

It was Montana, so Tabby was a little surprised when Logan shook his head.

Tabby walked in as Logan stood aside and surveyed the room. "Okay, she looks old enough not to put weird stuff in her mouth, drown in a wash bucket, or stick her fingers in electrical sockets, but let's look at strangle risks. Your blind strings should be put up out of reach."

Logan followed her pointing finger and obediently wound the strings up out of the way, reaching over the sleeping girl to get them. "I never would have thought of that," he whispered. Franzi didn't stir.

"The motorcycle is a crushing hazard, probably," Tabby said just as quietly. "Can you secure it to the wall so it can't fall on her? I know that dogs and pets aren't supposed to drink antifreeze, so is there anything toxic that should be sealed up?" The tools and fluids were all already put away—for a project clearly in progress, it was surprisingly tidy already. Logan found a bungee cord that he could sling around the bike and clip to a radiator. Tabby gave it a test poke and agreed that it would withstand at least a casual bump. "If she's really determined, she might be able to tip it."

They moved a mostly-empty bookcase over to cover a hole in the drywall where it looked like someone had kicked it in, more for aesthetics than for safety.

The kitchen was spic and span, if poorly stocked; the girl would have to climb up on the counters to get the knives, and the kitchen chairs were probably too heavy for her to move to stand on. "What do kids like to eat?" Logan wanted to know. "I've got some mac and cheese and bread. Do kids still hate vegetables?"

"I think it varies by kid. Have you asked her?"

"I asked what she likes," Logan said in despair. "But I only understand about half the words when she talks fast and I'm not even sure she was talking about food."

Tabby was standing close enough that she couldn't resist patting his arm comfortingly, and then it was hard to make herself stop. It was a very nice arm. "You're doing a good job," she said reassuringly.

"You don't have a lot to base that on," Logan reminded her.

Tabby had to laugh. "Well, no, but you're trying. That's more than some dads do. Just buy some vegetables and try them on her. You might be surprised." Should she ask if he had money problems? Nothing in the tiny apartment looked worth anything. Everything was secondhand at best, and many of the shelves were bare. Only about half the cabinets still had doors. "Is there anything you…need?"

"A job?" Logan said. "Sorry, that's probably not what you meant. And I wouldn't know what to do with her while I worked, even if I had work."

"Day care? I guess that's pretty expensive."

"And—" Logan shut his mouth around whatever he was going to say. "I've got to figure it out, I guess."

Tabby wasn't made of stone. He was earnest and clearly determined to do what was best for the poor orphaned little girl. "What line of work are you looking for?"

"Well, that's a big part of my problem. I haven't got any training or certification or work history," Logan said, shaking his head. "I've been…er…off the grid a while, and a few months each year of living in a car taking seasonal work isn't going to cut it with most employers."

Clancy Kennedy was a con man. Was Logan, too? He wouldn't be the first guy to go straight when faced with parenthood, and Tabby knew she was a sucker for someone trying to make a fresh start. "You just have to figure out how to spin your experience," Tabby said cheerfully. "You have some repair expertise, right?"

"I'm not sure how an indigent hobby mechanic looks on a resume."

Tabby considered. "How about *seasoned travel expert* and *specialist in small engine repair*. Did you clean the kitchen yourself? Boom. *Experienced household management*. Perhaps do not list interior decorating as a skill." She gestured at a poster of a girl in a very low-cut shirt serving beers.

Logan laughed, the way Tabby was hoping he would. "It's a…um… a friend's place. I sublet it on short notice."

"I hope you got a good deal," Tabby said, before she could stop herself.

"Thank you," Logan said, and Tabby realized that she hadn't actually stopped petting his arm when she tried to. He was very warm, and his look of amusement sobered until he was looking at her very intently, with the deepest, darkest eyes she'd ever seen. "Thank you, Tabby."

Tabby's hand froze as she realized what was wrong with his statement. "I didn't tell you my name."

Logan wasn't nearly the con man that his cousin Clancy was, and his face went from smoldering to panic in the space of just a breath.

Tabby cut him off when he started to sputter. "Did Clancy tell you who I was? The two of you are super *estranged*, I see. Is this some new kind of con? You ran out of identical horses and found a cute kid to play with my heartstrings? I haven't got any more *money* for you to steal." Something horrifying occurred to her. "Did you kidnap her? Are you keeping her for ransom?"

Her voice had raised as she backed away from Logan back into the living room. Should she cry for help? Call the police? She groped in her pocket for her phone.

"Wait!" Logan cried, following her out of the kitchen. "It's not like that! Hold on!" He reached for Tabby and she panicked, aborting her search for her phone and reaching for any weapon at hand. There were no handy swords on the walls, but Tabby snatched up the chair, hitting the table and knocking the play food everywhere.

The girl on the couch jerked awake at their noise, gave

an unholy wail of surprise and fear, struggled out of her blanket, and fell off the couch.

Tabby thought fleetingly of snatching up the girl and escaping the apartment, and then the little girl seemed to shiver in space, stretching into a long-legged foal.

The chair fell from Tabby's nerveless fingers and landed on her foot.

5

*L*ogan was sure things could not possibly get worse when he saw Tabby at his front door, but now he realized that was just a failure of his own imagination.

Franzi was in a blind panic, startled from sleep by the escalating fight, and she shifted out of instinct. The apartment was completely unknown. Logan was probably still a stranger to her. And Tabby was a newcomer, yelling and threatening him with a chair.

Tabby dropped the chair, right onto her own toes, and she bit back a cry as she hopped back into a half-filled bookshelf. Franzi leaped into the air.

Calm her down! Calm her! Calm her!

All of their careful childproofing had been for a short four-year-old with fingers, not a filly with long, breakable legs who tried to flee over the couch and out the window before ricocheting off the arm and into the motorcycle. It gave a clatter as the kickstand was knocked away and Logan was glad that he and Tabby had just tied it off to the wall because, while it might not have crushed her, it could have pinned a leg instead of just clipping her.

Franzi bolted from this new danger and tried to scramble behind the sagging easy chair that faced the couch. She was not quite four feet tall at the shoulder, and there was simply not enough space between the chair and the wall. She panicked as she couldn't find a place that felt safe.

Logan had to shut Tabby from his mind as she hissed colorful swearwords under her breath and gathered the chair back up as if she was a lion tamer. Logan ought to be panicking because Franzi had just exposed the secret of shifters in one fell swoop, but instinct was adamant that Tabby was not a danger, chair or not. The important thing now was getting Franzi soothed.

Logan's stallion wasn't helping at all, with his own animal panic. *Calm her! Calm her!!*

It would be easier if you weren't freaking out in my head, Logan pointed out.

Calm her!!

Logan knew that chasing Franzi would only make it worse so he went slowly and carefully to the center of the room, where he could sit, and she would have room to approach him.

She had her face stuffed behind the chair, but none of the rest of her would fit there, no matter how she struggled and kicked.

"Franzi," Logan called quietly. "It's okay. It's Uncle Logan and this is Tabby and no one is going to hurt you. You're okay. You're safe. Everything is fine."

The motorcycle, determined to make a liar out of him, fell the last few inches with a crash as the bungee cord slipped from the seat where it had been looped.

Tabby gave a squeak that turned into a hysterical

laugh, and she put the chair down with a thump and sat awkwardly down on it herself as if her legs had given out.

Franzi stopped kicking, but stood shivering in fear, not offering to pull her head out from behind the chair. She was a young filly, all lanky legs and anxiously flicking tail, her mane pale against her honey hide. She had four white socks and a blaze down her nose.

"Did your dad teach you the lullaby our mom sang?" Logan asked, not sure how else to start. "Pickles in the jar, tell me who you are…can you see the moon, you will be there soon?"

He didn't remember all the verses, it had been too long. "Something something something in your head. Pickles in the beer, tell me what you hear…can you see…" Surely it hadn't been *beer*. Logan stumbled through. "No, can you be…?"

Franzi lay down, her head still behind the chair. Should Logan go to try to comfort her?

No.

Logan wasn't sure what was instinct and what was his stallion; it was sometimes hard to tell them apart, but right now they were aligned. If he moved now, he would spook the girl.

He started over again. "Pickles in the jar, tell me who you are. Can you see the moon? You will be there soon. Pickles in the…soup? Glass? Dang, I don't remember the next words."

Franzi finally pulled her head out and whinnied impatiently.

When she realized she couldn't speak, she shifted, hanging back in the protected space beside the chair. "Pickles in your cheek. Sing a song of sleep." She had shifted with her dress, an impressive feat considering her age and how panicked she had been.

"Oh, that's good," Logan said. "You know the song better than I do! Thank you, Franzi."

He was rewarded with the barest hint of a tear-stained smile.

Stanza by stanza she crept out a little further, until Logan could have reached out and picked her up. He still didn't, letting her come of her own will to finally crawl right into his lap and go limp in his arms. He wrapped her up and rocked her gently. "I won't let anything hurt you," he promised. "You're safe here. I'll protect you."

"Not SUPOZE to be a horsey," she whispered in anguish. "Sorry." It sounded like *sowwy* in her childish lisp.

"It's okay," Logan promised. "You're safe. It's okay here."

Franzi clung to him and sobbed in relief.

Logan didn't realize that his chest could feel like this as he comforted her. It was as if his heart behind his ribcage was too big to fit there, as if he was softer and somehow still stronger than he'd ever been. Franzi was so complicated and precious and it was impossible that Logan had only known her a day and could be so completely in love with her.

Herd, his stallion said with a nicker of joy. *Our herd.*

"*That's* how you did it," Tabby said abruptly. Logan had almost forgotten that she was there. She *ought* to be there, like Franzi was supposed to be in his lap with her warm, comfortable weight as her crying slowed.

The momentary serenity vanished. Tabby wasn't dumb, and now that she knew that shifters were *possible*...

"That pretentious lock of white hair and your supernatural gracefulness. That smart, smart horse. That was *you*, you *sonuvabitch*."

6

*T*abby felt like an idiot, and at the same time, she was relieved to finally have answers.

When she had considered *magic, maybe?* as a possible explanation for Better Behave's disappearance, she had been thinking about witchcraft, not werewolves. (Werehorses?) Shapeshifting was nonsense, like love at first sight and free rides. Portals seemed more likely.

But now the world was upside down, and she'd just watched a little girl turn into a long-legged foal. It explained so much. Except…

"Why'd you do it? Why'd you screw *me* over?"

It was really hard to think of Logan as a jerk who would steal her entire life savings when he was cuddling a tearful little girl with trusting eyes. But the guilt in his face was unmistakable when he looked up over Franzi's curly head. He didn't try to deny his part, or excuse it.

"Money. You had it, we needed it."

Fury burned in Tabby's throat. "Did you think that maybe I needed it, too? Did you think that maybe I had a mortgage to pay, and bills and the bad end of a divorce that left me with even more debt than regret? I spent every fu—" Logan's niece was staring at her and Tabby swallowed the rest of what she was going to say. "You owe me a horse, Logan Kennedy."

Logan's arms tightened around Franzi.

He couldn't possibly think that Tabby meant *her*.

Tabby was stung that he might think she'd threaten a little kid. But blackmail was a thing, and Tabby should know. "I'm sure that child services would *love* to know about your checkered past," she said firmly. "I've got a dossier on you and your cousin that cost me a pretty penny. I still need a high-end horse. I have a bill of sale for you, and I expect to get my money's worth out of you, Mr. Kennedy."

Logan blinked at her in confusion. "You want me…to be a horse for you?"

"That's what I bought," Tabby said firmly. "I don't have any use for you as a man, but I have plenty of need for a good horse." She recognized the fib as she said it; she could think of *several* uses for Logan in human form, but she blustered on with a stream of consciousness as the idea occurred to her. "I have an empty place above the barn that's finished. You can do some basic labor around the ranch and help me fix up the outbuildings, and I'll let you live there in exchange for that. No stipend for your expenses and utilities aren't included, you're on your own for food and childcare and power. You can pay off your rather large outstanding debt by being what I bought in the first place."

Franzi was getting restless in Logan's arms and he released her. She seemed to have forgotten her earlier terror, and went to poke through the boxes of toy dishes and food that Tabby had scattered. She righted the boxes and busily started setting up a kitchen.

"You can't *prove* anything," Logan said smoothly, getting to his feet. "No one is going to believe that I can shapeshift into a horse if you tell them."

"I imagine that there are people out there who would be very interested in my story, and that you wouldn't love to suddenly be the center of their attention," Tabby bluffed, standing as well. Who *would* she tell? Cryptid-hunters? There were some popular video channels on the topic, like *Molly Flash*. She'd always figured they were impossible fantasies created by people trying to make a buck by being sensationalist.

Now she wasn't so sure. She pressed on before Logan could respond. "Maybe you can keep your secret, but I bet that's a lot harder now that you have a four-year-old. Do you want to always be watching over your shoulder, wondering when the press will descend, or would you like to raise your niece on a nice ranch just outside of Nickel City where an extra horse or two won't be noticed?"

"Tea?" Franzi tugged at Logan's arm and directed him to the couch where he obediently sat.

"I'd love a cup of tea, kitten," he said dazedly. Franzi skipped back to her makeshift kitchen and poured a cup of invisible liquid into a plastic flowered teacup. Tabby took a seat in the battered recliner. It seemed like the kind of chair you shouldn't ever look at with a blacklight but Tabby's knees were still shaking with shock and she didn't want to look weak by collapsing when they gave out.

"HOT!" Franzi cautioned. "Hot!" She blew on the plastic cup dramatically and handed it gingerly to Logan, who made a show of carefully taking it and pretending to drink.

A second cup came cautiously to Tabby. Unwilling to be outdone, Tabby took it with profuse gratitude and tasted it. "Hot!" she agreed. "Delicious. Can I have more sugar?"

Franzi gave a delighted giggle and nodded, dashing off with the cup to scoop pretend sweetener into it.

"Perfect," Tabby declared. "Now about our agreement…"

Logan met her eyes over his plastic cup and his gaze flickered between Franzi and Tabby.

Tabby was wise enough to know that if circumstances had been just a little different, he would be gone. By the time she came back with authorities—even assuming she could come up with a story to tell them—he would be long gone, under an assumed name in another state. It had taken her six months and a really expensive private investigator to track him this far, and if it weren't for Franzi, Logan would be on the run again, covering his tracks even better than before. But she had something *he* wanted—a place to raise a filly-shifting girl in safety.

"What *exactly* do you want me to do?" Logan asked. He gave his cup back to Franzi, who was bouncing in place as she waited. "All gone!" He leaned forward a little and gave Tabby an artfully smoldering look. "Does it have to be as a horse? I have other talents that could be…exploited."

Tabby wasn't immune to his dashing good looks or the intensity of his attention, but she only scowled at him. "Maybe we should go back to the original plan where you were going to be gelded."

Logan drew back and made a show of crossing his legs.

Tabby wondered how much she ought to explain. "I board and train horses and teach lessons at my ranch, but I…I recently had to start over from scratch. I bought *you* as my personal horse to qualify in jumping shows in order to build my branding and attract new clients. No one hires a trainer if they don't have a horse to show off."

Logan chuckled. Franzi shyly brought him another imaginary cup of tea and he gamely pretended to drink it. "It's a good thing this isn't real tea," he whispered to Tabby when the little girl had collected the second "all gone!" cup and gone back to the makeshift kitchen to make a new pot.

"Would you be peeing like a *racehorse?*" Tabby whispered back. She worried at once that she was too crude, but she was still high on adrenaline and punch drunk on pretend tea. She was also fully aware of exactly how hot Logan was, even without the added glamor of being a magical shapeshifter.

Fortunately, Franzi seemed oblivious to any tension between them, and she was content to continuously refill their cups, even as the novelty of the game ran thin for the grownups.

"Tell me more about shapeshifting," Tabby demanded as she pretend-drank her fourth cup. "Is it a phase of the moon thing? If you bite me, will I turn into a pony?" Oh no, now she was thinking about Logan biting her, and it wasn't an unpleasant idea. Tabby hoped that her flush wasn't obvious. "I mean, I'm guessing it's genetic. Was your mother a horse?" It came out sounding more insulting than she meant because she was flustered.

"My father was," Logan said. "A warmblood, like me. My mother was a circus trick-rider."

"Something I imagine was easier with a shapeshifter horse husband," Tabby observed, sipping more imaginary tea.

Franzi scolded her. "It's HOT! You have to ask for sugar!"

Tabby went through the song and dance of blowing on her tea and getting a scoop of sugar.

"You can't catch shifting through bites," Logan assured her.

Tabby felt a stab of disappointment, and she wasn't sure if it was because Logan wasn't offering to nibble her, or because this wasn't a chance for her to suddenly be a—

"What do you call yourselves? Werehorses?"

"Shifters," Logan explained. "We're shifters."

"Are there a lot of you? Are you all horses?"

"HOT!" Franzi told Logan, giving him a cup and waiting for him to blow on it and drink it down.

"Not a lot, no. We recognize each other when we meet, sort of a magical tingle that's part of our instinct, and I'll meet…maybe another shifter every week or month, depending on how many crowds I'm in. It's a numbers game. Depends on the density of humans."

Tabby tried to figure out how many people she met in a week. Not that many, working long hours every day on her ranch. She didn't get out much, and usually preferred horse company to human anyway.

"We aren't all horses," Logan went on. "You find all kinds, but it's impolite to ask, so I'm not really sure what's out there. I knew a guy who was a bear, and…ah…dated an otter shifter once." He patiently gave the cup back to Franzi and ruffled her hair.

Tabby told herself she was jealous of the otter shifter for being magical, not for dating Logan. Logan had probably dated *scads* of women, and maybe even a few guys, and she didn't care a bit.

Franzi's next delivery came with plates of plastic food, which Tabby gamely play-ate while she tried to figure out what else to ask. "I'd ask if you have references, but I already know all of them," she said thoughtfully.

"How did you find me?" Logan asked. "I thought we were—I was—better at covering my tracks."

"I hired a private investigator. I guess that people who make fake IDs have a price, if you know who to pay. I also asked around at the police department with both of your names and all the ones I found for Clancy."

"Shi—oh, heck, that's probably how child services finally tracked me down."

"Sorry," Tabby said sheepishly. She reminded herself that she shouldn't feel bad for ruining his life after what he'd done to her.

"I'm not."

"Not what?"

"Sorry."

Logan was looking tenderly at Franzi, who had taken the plates back to the table where one of the boxes had been designated a sink and was merrily washing all the dishes.

Tabby didn't know much about kids, but she thought that Logan was doing a pretty amazing job of being a brand new dad, and it was embarrassing how much that affected her. She swore she wouldn't be soft for a sob story, but Logan didn't seem to be trying to use it for leverage.

"So, what are you going to do?"

"I'd been thinking about getting certified as a mechanic anyway," Logan admitted, and he looked adorably abashed. "Maybe it's time I settled down and did that. Your place is an easy commute from Nickel City, which ought to be big enough to have an apprenticeship available. I could do that during weekdays and help you out on the weekends. I just…don't know what to do with Franzi."

"Isn't there a day care for shifters or something?" Tabby suggested.

"No, of course not," Logan scoffed. "There's no such thing."

7

*L*ogan stared suspiciously at his laptop screen. He'd been quite confident when he told Tabby the day before that there was no such thing as *a day care for shifters*, but instinct (and his ass of a stallion) had insisted that he look anyway.

A search for 'day care for shifters near Nickel City, Montana' unexpectedly brought up a barebones webpage that had as many photos of animals as it did children. And not just puppies and kittens, but…was that a bear cub and a *giraffe*?

The site was vague enough that it might have only been using stock images to pad out its gallery and lean into the cute and kitschy aesthetic all day cares seemed to have, but Logan was doubtful.

It did not actually have the word shifters anywhere on the page, despite the search results, but the underlying message was clear: it was a day care for *special* children, highly selective about their clientele, and they didn't specify what their criteria was. If it was for neurodivergent or disabled children, Logan guessed they would have been a lot more specific, and there were a lot of curiously-worded sentences that meant a lot more if you knew that people could change into animals.

"Would you like to go to Tiny Paws and play with other kids?" he asked Franzi.

Franzi was lying on the stained carpet, kicking her feet in the air. "I riding a BI-cycle!" she declared.

The facility accepted babies through kindergarten, and boasted a "very private play yard" and a "diverse, educational curriculum."

We provide loving instruction in all the childhood basics, including potty training, dressing, taking clothing, eating, reading, language, and social skills.

Taking clothing?

That could be a reference to shifting with clothing on. Some kids picked that up really easily, and Franzi seemed to have the knack for it, but Logan remembered his brother Steven's stubborn refusal to take his clothing with him. Their grandmother had often lamented about how expensive it was to keep him dressed because he split his seams when he shifted.

You're the one who should be doing this, Steven, Logan thought achingly. If he had been closer with his brother, maybe Franzi wouldn't have been alone for so long. Maybe, if he'd been in the right place at the right time, his brother and his wife wouldn't even have died. He still didn't know what had happened to them and vowed to find out.

I screwed everything up, he lamented.

Can we be done with this pity party? his stallion huffed impatiently. *We have our herd now, take care of it!*

Take care of it.

Logan picked up his phone and dialed the number from the webpage.

"Tiny Paws! This is Addison!"

The problem with phones is that there was no tingle of instinct to tell him if he was talking to a shifter.

"I'm interested in a day care for my…*special* daughter."

"What's your daughter's birthdate?"

Logan realized two things at once: he'd called Franzi his daughter by accident, and he had no idea when her birthday was. "Hang on," he said, frantically rifling through the paperwork the agency had given him. It had to be in here somewhere. "November 13. She's four. She's actually my niece."

If Addison found it suspicious that he'd had to look it up, she was polite enough not to mention it. "Does your niece have a *favorite animal*?"

It was an innocuous, if very odd question, but Logan knew exactly what she meant.

"Horsey. Ah, her favorite animal is a horse." It was a safe answer.

"We *do* have an opening for a child of that age," Addison said very carefully. "Perhaps we should *meet* and see if she would be a good *fit*."

That tracked for a day care for shifters. She would want to see Franzi in person to verify that she was a shifter.

"I'm over in Billings, is there a good time or day?"

"We're closed over the weekend, could you make it by on Monday between ten and noon?"

"Yes," Logan said. "Yes, that would be fine. Thank you." He gave Addison his name—his real name, which felt odd—and some brief details about Franzi, thanked her again, and hung up.

Franzi had stopped pedaling and was gazing at him with big curious eyes. "Not SUPOZE to be a horsey," she reminded him.

"Maybe you can," Logan said hopefully. It would be nice to have a place to grow up where it was safe to shift.

He thought wistfully of Tabby's forest-hemmed ranch. A few extra horses would never be noticed.

He made a second call, to confirm that there was a union shop in Nickel City that offered apprenticeships, and what the terms were. He agreed to bring in his resume on Monday morning and hung up feeling hopeful.

There was just one more phone call he needed to make, and it filled him with more nervousness than either of the prior ones.

Before he called Tabby, he made Franzi a grilled cheese sandwich, cut sideways, and piled her plate full of pickles.

While Franzi was fastidiously making stacks of the pickle chips and keeping their juice from her sandwich, Logan stepped out into the hallway. There was an empty beer can tossed casually down opposite from his door, and a few candy wrappers. The carpet was so stained that Logan couldn't have guessed what color it was originally supposed to be, and there were places where chewed up gum had been ground into it. Franzi deserved a better place to grow up.

"Swiftwater Ranch," Tabby answered after a few moments. She sounded breathless.

"If your offer is still on the table, I'll take it," Logan blurted.

She was silent for so long that Logan hesitantly added, "This is Logan Kennedy," in case she had more than one offer on the table.

"My horse," Tabby snorted. "I know."

Logan was sure that being called her horse shouldn't feel as good as it did. He told himself that he was just relieved that they weren't starting from scratch with her.

"If you'd prefer alternate service terms, I'm still amenable to that arrangement," Logan added archly.

Tabby gave a shout of laughter. "Keep dreaming,

stud," she told him. "Strictly platonic horse services and general labor are all I need." She sobered. "I've got ground rules."

"I'm listening."

"No parties, no overnight visitors without prior permission. I'll provide and fix appliances, you don't trash the place or flush anything weird down the septic system. No drugs, whether it's decriminalized or not, and no heavy drinking. I'm not your babysitter and I'm not your mother. I expect you to maintain a professional demeanor on my property at all times. No joyriding while I'm on your back; you're my demo horse, and I expect you to set the bar. Other duties will be as needed. There are some rentals I've been wanting to finish and I've got a garden that needs water and weeding. We can agree on exact hours and I'll have a contract for you to sign. With your *real* name."

Logan felt a rush of relief. Tabby still wanted him.

He was pretty sure that it was only because of pity for Franzi, but for the first time in a long time, it felt like he was coming home.

"I solemnly swear to respect your person and your property, and…I'm very grateful for this opportunity," Logan said humbly. "I can be there on Sunday. On Monday, I'm applying for a spot for Franzi at a day care in Nickel City and I'm putting my resume in at a union shop for an express technician position that can flex into an apprenticeship. It sounds like they are pretty desperate, so I have a good chance."

"That sounds great," Tabby said, her voice unexpectedly warm and encouraging. "You've gotten a lot done!"

"I took your resume advice," Logan chuckled. "I'm sure they'll be blown away by the *Experienced Household Management* part."

"And the day care?" Tabby asked carefully.

"A *very special* day care. I'll know more on Monday for sure, but instinct suggests that it will work out."

"Must be nice having a magical power to tell you the right thing to do," Tabby said wistfully.

"It only works when I'm actually listening to it," Logan said, and then he stiffened because he realized that underneath the humming excitement of talking to Tabby was another layer of anxiety. "Sorry, gotta go!" he cried, just as there was a tremendous crash from inside the apartment.

"Good lu—" Tabby said as Logan hung up and jammed his phone into his pocket to burst back into the apartment and find Franzi standing on a chair by the kitchen counter looking down at the toolbox she'd managed to push off onto the floor.

"Sorry!" she cried tearfully. "I wanted more pickles!"

"It's okay," Logan said, kneeling to collect his tools. There were some new scratches in the linoleum. "It's okay, Franzi. I wasn't going to get my deposit back, anyway. Don't sweat it."

"Done swept it," Franzie agreed, climbing down from the chair.

8

*D*espite specifying that she wasn't interested in being Logan's babysitter, Tabby was delighted to find that one of the horse-crazy teenagers she taught, Letisha, was willing to watch a four-year-old girl on the weekend in exchange for extra lessons, which would free Tabby up to train with Logan and put him in nearby shows.

Everything *seemed* to be falling perfectly into place and Tabby wished she had supernatural instinct to tell her if it really *was* working out, or if she was just being her usual optimistic self, oblivious to the fact that she was walking straight into another disaster.

You're too impulsive, her mother would say. *It's not that trouble finds you, it's that you go find it.*

Certainly it had been impulsive of her to offer Logan a place to stay. But he was clearly trying very hard to be a good dad, and the place he was living was no kind of space for a four-year-old girl who could change into a horse.

And it had been impulsive of her to go see him in the first place.

Tabby hadn't been able to shake off the memory of that brilliant, beautiful horse, and she'd hoped that she would be able to get more out of Logan about his cousin in person that she could over the phone; he was clearly the kind to disappear at the drop of a hat.

It was hard to wrap her head around the fact that he was magical on top of mysterious.

Which begged the question: was it unethical to ride a human-shifting horse in a competition? Was it any different than buying a horse that had already been trained and riding it in shows to demonstrate her own skill? Tabby was confident that she was a good trainer and rider, and she loathed taking shortcuts, but she didn't have money to buy a new horse and use it to prove herself, having lost it all on Logan. Her finances were more dire than she'd implied to Logan, and she dreaded losing the ranch altogether.

She didn't have time to second-guess any of her decisions. It was a gorgeous spring morning, and there was rain coming. If she didn't get her starts into the garden after her morning barn rounds, she'd miss her opportunity to do that without getting soaked.

She checked her watch when she heard the truck pull up at the gate several hours later. She'd forgotten to wear a hat and probably should have put sunscreen on a while ago; she could feel the heat of the spring sun on her bare arms and the nape of her neck. The base of her back burned from bending over for so long.

Tabby had left the gate unlocked because she was expecting the company and when she walked to the curve in the driveway to meet him, Logan had already pulled through and was shutting it behind him. Not all visitors were so courteous.

Tabby made herself not stare as Logan got out of the

truck in front of her house. His pants were tighter than strictly required, she thought, and his T-shirt left little to the imagination. His boots were work-worn, not fashionably new. She brushed the dirt off of her hands on her jeans self-consciously. A hat would have saved her from sunburn *and* covered the messy mop of her hair, but it was too late to scurry inside and put it on now without looking like she was trying to impress him.

Which she certainly wasn't.

He tipped his own hat to her and went around to open his passenger door and lift Franzi out of her car seat.

He tossed the little girl up in the air with ease and she giggled and clutched at Logan before he settled her against his hip with an arm around her. Her long legs dangled on either side of him and she looked perfectly comfortable being held as she stared around at the ranch in interest.

Tabby told her uterus to stop squealing and went to greet them briskly. "Let me show you the place you'll be staying," she said without preamble. "For *now*."

She marched them over to the barn and up the outside steps. Franzi insisted on climbing them herself and Logan hovered behind her, clearly trying not to micromanage her efforts. Tabby watched them from the landing above and had more stern words for her libido. She was absolutely not going to take Logan's alternate services offer just because he was heart-meltingly smitten with his niece and a hundred times sexier because of it.

"It's not a lot," she said, unlocking the door for them. "I've been planning to set it up as an Airbnb, but I hadn't gotten around to it yet. You'll be responsible for any damages, of course."

It was a tiny apartment with two tiny bedrooms, but it had airy windows with blue checked curtains and a view of the mountains. "It's got furniture, but I don't have sheets or towels. The place doesn't come with maid service. There's laundry in the house, but ask before you use it because the septic system is pretty old and it can't handle that many loads in one day. The well water is fine to drink, but has a slight mineral flavor. If you don't like it, you can buy bottled on your own dime."

Tabby led them through the space, opening cabinets to show the storage space. Franzi didn't offer to touch anything, looking around with big eyes.

"This will be your room, kitten," Logan said of the slightly larger room. They each had double beds with just enough room to walk around three sides, a narrow dresser, and a bedside table.

"My room?" Franzi said hopefully. She had a finger in her mouth, so it came out *woom*. "All mine?"

Tabby met Logan's eyes over her curly head and they shared a little heart-shredded moment at her uncertainty.

"All yours," Logan assured her. "Let's go get your suitcases."

Despite her insistence that she wasn't a mother, housekeeper, or babysitter, Tabby also couldn't let Logan carry all of their things up the stairs without helping. "Do you have another truck load to get?" she asked. The bed of the truck was full of boxes—mostly liquor boxes—and the motorcycle that had fallen over in his living room.

"This is it," Logan said. "I move pretty regularly and don't have a lot of stuff."

"Plus, you probably don't need much as a horse," Tabby observed. She tried not to peer too curiously into the boxes where their flaps were loose. "You have a good stock of Sunshine Wine, I see," she teased, picking one up from the bed of the truck.

Logan flushed. "Liquor boxes are made to carry heavy

things, so they make great moving boxes, and they give them away free."

"I have a suitcase," Franzi said proudly, trying in vain to lift it.

Logan found a pillow for her to carry up the stairs, while he somehow managed a heavy box and both her suitcases.

They had to go at Franzi's stair speed, which was agonizingly slow, one hand reaching up to the rail, the other dragging her pillow.

"Have you lived here long?" Logan asked, pausing to admire the view out over the ranch while he took each step a minute apart.

Tabby, on the steps behind him with entirely too good a view of his ass, wished she had taken a shower before they got here. She was hot and sweaty from working all morning, and her muscles already ached before she tried to show off by carrying two heavy stacked boxes. "I've been here five years, but it's only been mine for a year."

"Whose was it before that?"

Tabby considered her words carefully. "My husband and I bought it together the year that we got married." She wished that Franzi would go faster; she was sweating and the boxes were digging into her arms. "When we divorced, I kept the ranch and the debt and he got the horses, all our clients, and his hot secretary."

"That doesn't sound like a fair split."

"He had a realtor friend, Veronica Chase, who got a shady appraisal that jacked up the value of the ranch when I insisted on keeping it in the settlement. Later, she tried to offer me way too little for it, and when I told her to get off my land, she warned me she'd get it for a song when I lost it to foreclosure."

Logan glanced back at her and Tabby flushed because

she was still staring at his butt. "Sorry," he said gruffly. "I'm glad you kept it. Your ex sounds like a jerk."

Tabby shrugged. "He got what he deserved. He was married to his secretary for six months before he cheated on her. She was smart enough to get a really good lawyer, so he got taken to the cleaners."

"Good."

Tabby told herself that she didn't need Logan's approval and that it shouldn't feel so nice. "There's a secondhand store in Nickel City if you need anything else," she said, finally reaching the landing and squeezing inside to drop her boxes on the kitchen counter. She rubbed at the red marks across her forearms.

"I've got a coffee pot and a toaster," Logan said. "Don't need much more."

He took the suitcases to Franzi's new room. "You want to unpack while we get the rest?" he asked her.

Franzi nodded eagerly, and Logan unlatched the suitcases for her before clattering quickly down the stairs with Tabby, both of them relieved to have more speed than a snail. "It's supposed to rain this afternoon," Tabby warned him. "Do you want to put the motorcycle in the stable?"

"That would be great," Logan said, and Tabby took another two boxes and didn't wait for him to go first.

She paused at the landing as he came up, easily carrying four stacked boxes. They must be light, Tabby decided. He wasn't straining in the least. Or maybe it was a shifter thing.

Franzi was lining up a half dozen well-worn stuffed animals on her bare mattress. All of the drawers were pulled out of the dresser and the suitcases were empty. "My room!" she said happily, and she slammed the door when she went to close it. "Sorry!"

The door opened and shut several more times while Tabby and Logan brought up the last load.

There was a rumble of distant thunder and a rush of cool, damp air through the open windows as Tabby put her box on the couch—there weren't that many boxes, but the kitchen counter was very small. "We'd better get the motorcycle into the barn if we're going to," she cautioned. "And I want to check on the horses. Trudy gets twitchy with loud noises."

"You okay here for a few minutes?" Logan asked through Franzi's closed door.

"I'm okay!" Franzi sang. "I'm in my room!"

Tabby smiled foolishly all the way down the stairs and went to open up the big double doors as Logan brought the truck around.

He backed up tight to the doors and three curious heads turned their way.

"You've got a few horses already," Logan observed as he slid a battered aluminum ramp from the side of the truck bed.

"Those are my boarders," Tabby explained fondly. "The pinto is Oreo, and Angus is the shaggy brute of a pony. His owner gets a break on board to let me do lessons on him. Truly Spoiled might give you a run for your money for worst name on papers, but her barn name is Trudy and she's a sweet old lady enjoying her retirement."

Logan groaned. "Please give me a better name than Better Behave," he begged, vaulting up into the truck instead of using the ramp. Tabby told herself that he probably wasn't doing it to show off.

"No promises," she said.

He didn't start the motorcycle, only put it in neutral and pushed it down the ramp. Tabby opened a stall for him and stood aside. "I'll charge you extra rent if I start running out of stall space," she warned. "But it will probably be a while before I get to that point."

It started to rain just as they closed the door, and Tabby found herself lamenting her sweaty, disheveled state again because she was standing very close to Logan looking out at it. "I'm glad I got the starts in the garden," she said inanely. "This way I won't have to water them."

"Have you got a honey-do list for me to start in on this week?" Logan asked.

"I'm calling it my horsey-do list," Tabby said with a sideways look. "It's getting pretty long. And I'm not adding anything hinky," she reminded him, because she was terribly aware of how close he was standing and what that was doing to her.

"Purely platonic," Logan agreed, but he said it with a sly grin that suggested he knew *exactly* how he affected her.

"This was supposed to be a dude ranch," Tabby explained, trying to convince her cheeks not to flush. "Sort of a country escape for city folk who wanted to be around horses and mountains. But the bunkhouses were never finished and I couldn't do that on my own or afford to hire a contractor. If I can fix up some of them up well enough, I can list them as short term rentals and supplement my horse boarding business. I thought I'd include a free lesson with each 3-day stay, and offer trail rides. People might even bring their own horses. It's such a gorgeous place and the trails are amazing. There are miles of them. And there's space for a big garden, and pasture for the horses." She recognized that she was babbling and made herself stop talking. "It's...just got a long ways to go," she said haltingly.

"I can see it," Logan said softly.

For a moment, Tabby couldn't, because her eyes had welled with tears. "Sorry," she mumbled, ashamed.

"For having a dream?" Logan asked. He looked like he wanted to touch her and Tabby longed for it at the same time that she was glad he was respecting her space.

"You probably don't want to leave Franzi alone too long," she reminded him after a space of silence. "The rain has let up a little; we should probably make a dash for it."

They both made a show of bracing for the run and Tabby was still laughing when she got to her porch, damp and feeling dangerously giddy.

She was going to have to be careful with her heart, Tabby realized as she stomped off her boots on the mat and sobered. It would be really easy to fall for a funny guy who could be a horse and had a sense of humor and honor. But he'd already taken her for a ride once, and she wasn't going to be fooled twice. No matter how handsome he was, or how magical.

9

*L*ogan woke up in a strange bed to a strange sensation.

He was being stared at.

He'd left his bedroom door propped open so that he could hear if Franzi got scared at night and called for him, even though he'd closed *her* door because fire safety had been drilled into him. She stood like a little shadow in his doorway now, with big, luminous eyes.

The sun was already starting to come up, streaming straight through the cheerful curtains, though Logan's clock said it was just before six in the morning. There were sounds in the barn below that indicated that Tabby was up and feeding the horses.

"Good morning," he said gently. "Did you sleep well?"

He certainly had.

The ranch was quiet compared to the apartment in Billings. No distant alarms or arguments had disturbed his sleep, there were no slamming doors or stomping feet from floors above to startle him awake. The horses below rattled their water buckets a few times, stamped and nickered, but the sounds were muffled. He woke a few times to listen for Franzi, but instinct lulled him back to sleep almost at once.

Franzi didn't answer, only continued to observe him quietly.

"Are you excited to see the day care today?" Logan asked. Was she scared? Did she think that he would leave her again so soon? What was going on behind those quiet eyes?

"I'm hungry."

Logan chuckled and threw off his blanket. He only had one set of sheets, which had gone on Franzi's bed. "Let's go make a special breakfast," he said. "I found a can of corned beef hash when we were moving."

There was no bread or eggs to have with it, but he did have a box of Saltines, and Franzi ate with relish, swinging her legs in the tall chair. He'd have to find a booster seat or a thick cushion, Logan thought. Fat telephone books weren't a thing anymore, like they'd been when he was a kid.

"Can I have milk?" Franzi asked.

That was another thing Logan would have to see about getting. "I'll go shopping today," he promised.

It was much later than he wanted to leave when they were finally ready; he continued to underestimate how long it took Franzi to do anything. Getting dressed was agonizingly slow. Going to the bathroom took so long he wondered if he should go in after her. Brushing her hair caused so much crying and distress that he gave up before it was properly finished, sure he was doing it wrong.

He picked her up on one hip and carried her down the stairs rather than wait for her to take each step one by one, and buckled her into the rain-washed truck.

The Montana spring morning smelled amazing, and Logan rolled the windows down as they drove to Nickel City.

It was easy to find the day care on a touristy little street just a block from what passed as downtown. It looked like a gold rush saloon, and the windows in front were covered in translucent tissue paper. It was harder to find parking, and then Franzi wanted to dawdle, so Logan was pressing the button at the locked front door much later than he'd hoped to be, nearly at noon.

"Tiny Paws, how can I help you?"

"Logan Kennedy," he said into the box. "I'm here with my niece, Franzi." Should he apologize for running late? It was still a few minutes to noon. Franzi was tugging at his hand because she wanted to touch a tree that was just out of reach but Logan kept a grip on her. The last thing he needed was to have her run out in traffic.

"Come on in, Mr. Kennedy." The door gave a welcoming little burble as it unlocked, and Logan pushed it open.

There was a long narrow entryway the length of the building front, crowded with cubbies and benches. Dozens of miniature rain boots and sneakers marched along the space, and a cartoon of a bear with weirdly human toes asked everyone to take off their footwear. The sounds of children talking and playing were a background drone.

"Let's take off our shoes," Logan said, sitting on the bench. It was short and narrow, definitely sized for children.

Franzi shook her head and wrapped her arms around herself. Logan's heart sank. He didn't want to have an argument in the lobby of the day care. He was still figuring out how far to push Franzi, and how to balance making her do stuff with letting her have some autonomy. For the most part, he let her have her way, because he didn't want to be a horrible new authoritarian in her life.

"I'm taking off my boots," he said, making a show of wrestling the first one off. "I hope my socks aren't stinky!"

Franzi giggled at that.

"Here comes the other boot!" Logan said cheerfully. "Whew! It feels nice to wiggle my toes! Now it's your turn!"

Franzi's little smile froze into a grimace. "No."

Logan cast desperately for some kind of leverage, then leaned forward. "It's because you don't have toes, isn't it!"

Franzi's brow furrowed in confusion.

Logan nodded sagely. "You don't want anyone to know you don't have toes."

"I have toes!" Franzi protested.

"Prove it!"

Franzi stared at him, then heaved a sigh and plopped bonelessly down on the floor to pull off her sneakers and wiggle her toes at him.

"You do have toes!" Logan exclaimed. "Wow! How many do you have?"

Franzi giggled, then sobered and Logan realized that someone was watching them from the end of the entryway, where a baby gate separated them from another room.

It was an older woman who had clearly witnessed their entire exchange, based on her broad grin. She had blue-tipped, gray-streaked pony-tails and a pleasant round face that showed lines of humor and patience.

But she wasn't a shifter.

Logan had a stab of alarm and dismay. Was he wrong about this place? Could he trust Franzi in a day care for ordinary children? All of his plans suddenly seemed very precarious and he was surprised at the depth of his worry. He'd never bothered having plans before, and it was unsettling how much he wanted them to work out.

"You must be Mr. Kennedy," the woman said as Logan stood up and herded a reluctant Franzi towards her. She extended a hand that Logan shook firmly. There was still no tingle of shifter recognition.

Would you stop freaking out? his stallion scoffed. *Everything is fine.*

"This is my niece, Franzi—Frances Kennedy." *November 13*, Logan reminded himself. Her birthday was November 13. What else was he supposed to know about her? He wished he'd thought to bring all the paperwork from child services.

The woman smiled warmly down and offered Franzi her hand. "Hi Franzi. I'm Cherry."

Franzi gave her the most reluctant hand shake that Logan had ever witnessed and then went to hide behind Logan.

Cherry didn't seem bothered by her shyness, but she also didn't step aside to invite them into the day care. "Do you like painting, Franzi?"

Franzi nodded against the back of Logan's leg. Logan made a note to see if he could pick up some paints when he got milk and eggs and whatever else you fed children.

Another woman in a rainbow skirt appeared in the entrance behind Cherry and relief flooded through Logan. She was definitely a shifter, and the toddler that she held was also. She and Cherry traded approving nods and Cherry opened the gate.

"I'm Addison," the rainbow-skirted woman said. Her hands were too busy with the squirming toddler to shake. "Come on in!"

Logan didn't know what to expect from an ordinary day care, let alone one for shifters, and he was momentarily overwhelmed.

There were children everywhere, crawling, careening, and perched on the low furniture around the open room. Everything was bright and loud, reflected in tall mirrors that must be left over from a time when the place was a bar. There were short bookcases crowded with toys and books, lumpy beanbags, colorful carpets, and a row of cages holding class pets.

It all smelled faintly like bleach, glue, sawdust, and baby powder.

Logan's senses prickled. Not all of the children were shifters, but most of them were, and it was downright uncanny to be in a room with so many of them. Outside of his immediate family, it was rare to run into more than one at a time.

He also towered above *everyone* in the room. It was like being a giant.

Franzi clutched at his knees, staring around in wonder.

"We're about to have lunch," Cherry said. "Would Franzi like to join us and then we can go over our paperwork?"

"I'm hungry," Franzi said shyly.

Addison managed to speak over the din of the children without sounding like she was shouting. "Time to eat, everyone! Put your toys in time out and get your lunch bags!"

The chaos of the room changed in tenor. Some of the kids protested the change of activity and some of them shrieked in excitement and ran for their cubbies. A baby cried, and one of the children tripped over onto their face. They bounced back up without complaint.

"I didn't think to pack her a lunch," Logan said, chagrined. How was there so much that he didn't know?

"We've got a few emergency meals for kids in case they forget them," Cherry said. "Does she have any food allergies?"

"I hope not," Logan said, then wondered if that betrayed his sheer ignorance. Surely Mrs. Gravis would have warned him about them? He laughed so it would look like a joke.

"Have a seat anywhere," Cherry invited.

The tables and chairs were toddler short. With effort, Logan persuaded Franzi to let go of his legs and sit in one of the chairs, and pulled up his own beside her. Cherry brought her a lunch pack of cheese, meat, and crackers, as well as a Mandarin orange and a cup of water.

Franzi was the subject of curiosity and stares, but she refused to look at anyone else as she ate. Every time Logan tried to shift his weight in the uncomfortably tiny chair, she looked at him in panic. Was this a terrible idea? Would she be horribly unhappy here?

Logan tried to make conversation. "That looks yummy," he said. "Are you going to stack the cheese on top of the cracker?" He peeled the mandarin for her.

Then a girl about Franzi's age took a shy seat opposite from her. She had shoulder-length straight black hair and Asian features, and wore a ruffled pink shirt with a sequined unicorn on it. She didn't say a word, but after a few silent bites of her bagged lunch, she offered a raisin across the table.

Franzi glanced at Logan doubtfully and he smiled encouragingly. She accepted the raisin with a mumbled thank you. After a few quiet bites, she offered a segment of her orange in return, all without ever making eye contact.

The classroom didn't quiet much with the meal, and Logan watched several minor disasters unfold; one of the boys tipped an entire pitcher of water over, and a baby in a high chair shifted into a baby owl and slid out of one of the leg holes. She was quickly recaptured, dressed, and returned to the chair.

"Fingers and feet," Addison reminded the girl, refilling her tray with cereal. "Fingers and feet!"

Franzi forgot to eat, watching this happen. "Not SUPOZE to be a horsey," she murmured.

"You can be here," Logan said.

The girl across the table was staring at Franzi with big eyes. "Are you a horse?"

Franzi was surprised into looking straight at her. She didn't answer, but nodded slowly, and was rewarded with a slow smile.

"I'm a *unicorn*," the little girl said proudly, to Logan's surprise. "A *Chinese* unicorn. I can *fly*!"

Franzi stared and forgot to be bashful. "Can you show me?"

"We have to eat before we can play in the yard," the girl told her solemnly, and both of them fell on the remainder of their food.

"I have *never* seen Tara eat that fast before," Addison said to Logan as he helped wipe the crumbs up off the table. Franzi didn't seem to even remember that he was there as the girl took her by the hand and led her out the back of the classroom. "Cherry's in her office with your paperwork!"

Cherry's office was small and tidy, but the chair across from her desk was comfortably adult-sized. She handed Logan several forms and a rate sheet that made him gulp. He'd been living frugally since he parted ways with Clancy, but he didn't have enough to cover this for long. He hoped that the mechanic hired him, because even with free rent, he was going to run out of funds in a month or two.

"I understand that you are Franzi's uncle," Cherry said, inviting Logan to explain.

"I'm her legal guardian," Logan assured her. *For now.*

Cherry paused, but didn't pry when Logan didn't volunteer more. "Your registration is month-to-month, payment in advance. If she won't be attending, we request that you check in as a courtesy, but there's no prorate for days that you miss. She needs to bring a bottle of water, snacks and a bagged lunch each day. Nothing that needs to be microwaved, please. We ask that personal toys be left in her cubby so they don't get mixed up. We also ask that you have two changes of clothes here, we have a higher rate of attrition than most day cares."

Logan chuckled. "I imagine so."

"Is she potty trained?"

Logan nodded.

"Can she shift with her clothing?"

"Apparently." Logan knew he wasn't making a great impression. He was trying to fill out forms at the same time. How much did Franzi weigh? Less than a fifty-pound sack of concrete but more than a twenty-pound turkey. How tall was she? More than a yardstick?

"How long has Franzi been with you?"

"Five days," Logan said, suddenly overwhelmed. "Five of the longest days of my life."

Logan realized that his hands were clenching over the forms when Cherry reached over her desk and kindly patted them. "No parent in the history of the world has ever thought that they were truly prepared. You're doing fine."

"Do you have kids?" Maybe her kids were shifters, which would explain why she'd started a day care for them.

But Cherry shook her head and Logan thought that her understanding smile took a little hint of grief.

Logan wasn't going to pry. He knew what it was like to have secrets.

10

It felt wrong to leave Tiny Paws without Franzi, but the little girl didn't seem to mind that Logan was going away without her. His assurances that he would be back to get her soon were shrugged off as Franzi squatted to play dolls with her new self-proclaimed unicorn friend. Logan had never heard of a unicorn shifter, but he supposed it was possible.

Logan caught himself watching for traffic hazards as he walked the way he never had before, and several times automatically reached for a little shadow that wasn't there.

Our filly is fine, his stallion said carelessly. *We can frolic without her for a while!*

But there was more work to do before there was time for frolicking. Logan left his truck in its hard-won parking place and walked to the shop he'd talked to on the phone. It was a busy place, and loud, but after watching from the open bay for a few minutes, he was convinced that it was working like a well-oiled machine, pun intended.

"You got a car, you can pull up to any open bay and we'll work you in when we can," one of the technicians working under a big van called to him. "We're a little shorthanded today, so it might be a bit of a wait!"

"I'm here to see Mason," Logan called back. "I talked to him on the phone about a job."

The technician wiped his hands on his shop-branded apron and Logan got a tingle of instinct as he left the car to come shake Logan's hand. This man was a shifter, too.

"I'm Mason."

Logan greatly approved of a boss that did his own grunt work. The handshake itself was a test, and there was a little flicker of recognition between them as Logan felt a wave of relief. He was in the right place at the right time.

"While this beast drains its oil, I'll have a look over your resume and ask some questions," Mason said, leading him into the office.

Logan gave him the fresh-printed copy.

Well, fresh except for the red jam fingerprints that Franzi had helpfully left in the margins. Logan hadn't had time to find a place to reprint it; it wasn't sticky now, but it was slightly tinted.

Mason's big fingers left new oil stains on it anyway. "Some gaps here," he observed mildly.

It's a trap! his stallion shrieked unnecessarily. Logan wasn't sure if he was reacting to instinct, or to Mason's shifter presence. Sometimes his stallion got twitchy about predators. Instinct was sizzling, pressing on him to be… Logan tried to analyze the impulse. He knew that if he mis-stepped here, he'd be shooting down his whole plan. When he thought about using one of the carefully crafted stories that he usually used, there was a twang of misgiving.

"I had a footloose life of crime and passion," he said frankly. "My brother's daughter got orphaned and now I'm going straight and making a life to support her."

His stallion wasn't convinced that was the right answer, but Mason only raised an eyebrow. "Any felonies?"

"Nothing they could pin on me," Logan said with absolute honesty.

Mason gave a bark of laughter. "This your legal name?"

"Yes, sir."

"Why an auto shop instead of a bagger or a burger flipper?"

Logan's stallion gave a snort of outrage at the idea.

"Union opportunities," Logan said. "I got a little girl to get through college now. And I have a knack with machinery."

"You know you'd be starting as a scrub, right? It would be oil changes and tire switch outs for minimum wage until you'd worked up to a mentorship." Mason had brown eyes that were almost gold and they were assessing him with an unsettling directness.

"Everyone starts somewhere," Logan agreed, stifling his horse's wordless protest about their stolen dignity. "I'm not too proud to get dirty and I learn fast."

"If I run a background check and call these references, that going to be a problem?"

"Probably not a deal breaker," Logan said mildly. "Nothing they can tell you that I wouldn't."

Mason settled back in his chair. "Instinct suggests that I give you a chance," he said, glancing at his open door. "I could use another set of hands around here, and shifter strength is an asset. Anything else I should know?"

"I'll need weekends off for my second job," Logan said.

That got him a shout of laughter, then Mason sobered. "You mean that?"

"College is expensive," Logan said. "And I've got debts to settle."

Mason regarded him across the table and appeared to be having a conversation in his own head. "I think you'll fit in here," he said with a nod. "We'll do a month on trial and see what you pick up. Come in tomorrow at eight."

As they both stood, Logan reached out to shake his hand. "I appreciate it."

We should be the one in charge, his stallion complained as Logan left. *We are better than anyone else at everything.*

Your towering ego doesn't pay the bills, Logan pointed out.

His next stop was the general store, because corned beef hash and saltines with jam didn't satisfy all the food groups.

He stood in the aisle and stared at the array of kids' food in consternation. Everything was brightly packaged and screamed of health and flavor and favorite cartoon characters. Did Franzi like Disney princess applesauce or My Little Pony cheese sticks? Were they better than the generic branded ones?

After filling his cart, Logan did math and then did a lap of the store putting things back. He still needed to get her some new clothes and a few toys. He could do without sheets for a while longer, probably, and he could subsist on noodles and ketchup even if he wanted to get the organic sauce for Franzi. A cheap set of non-toxic paints and a pad of paper were deemed critical.

His stallion had distracting opinions about everything, insisting on only the best; he had a shaky understanding of money or the street value of kids shoes, but he was sure that a filly of theirs was entitled to the top shelf.

"She's *four,*" Logan told him under his breath. "She doesn't care if her pants are Gucci as long as they are pink." At least, Logan hoped she liked pink, because most of her wardrobe was, and apparently most of the current options for girl's clothing. He reluctantly put back a dozen full-priced outfits and vowed to find the secondhand store that Tabby had mentioned.

To his surprise, both at the general store and the charity store, Hand-Me-Down, he ran into shifters, defying the population density that he had described to Tabby. He met their eyes and gave a little nod of recognition, then pushed his cart past them.

Hand-Me-Down was a treasure trove, with an array of furniture in stages of disrepair. Logan took some measurements with his hands to check when they got home, but resisted the cherry bookshelf. It was a little out of his budget, and he'd gotten rid of most of his books several moves ago anyway. But didn't Franzi need a place to store her toys? Her room wasn't big enough for the toy chest he found, with an adorable cartoon town map hand-painted on the top that was perfect for staging adventures, but he had to buy the wooden rocking horse that was hiding behind it. It would need a good sanding and paint job, but it was cheap, and too apt.

Our filly's filly! his horse chortled.

He tucked the rocking horse into the back of the truck with the groceries and went to pick up Franzi.

11

"You know your way around power tools," Logan said admiringly.

"I've had to do everything myself for so long that I've forgotten what it's like to have good help," Tabby said, then wished she hadn't, because Logan grinned at her like she'd just made a dirty joke and she was pretty sure that she had.

Each drywall sheet went up easily with two people, and Logan was strong enough to hold it in place while Tabby tacked it onto the studs with a screw gun. The bunkhouse was finally looking like a dwelling, and not a hollow shell with open walls.

"I can do the plaster and painting myself," she said, fighting back the heat in her ears as she finished the screw pattern. She was absolutely not going to give Logan any encouragement, and she reminded herself that he was clearly just the flirty, flattering type. He'd look at anyone in tight jeans the way he was looking at her. "I just needed some muscle to get the boards into place."

Logan had already moved to stack the sawhorses that

had held the drywall sheets and pick up the saw they'd used to cut out the electricity penetrations.

Penetrations.

Tabby caught herself lingering over the word.

Why were so many construction terms so *filthy?* She was a grown woman who could keep herself from being distracted by a hot guy, no matter how long it had been. She sank a screw too deep and swore under her breath. She could fix it with joint compound.

By the time she'd finished putting all the screws in, Logan had wound up the extension cord and put the saw away. He had the box for the screw gun waiting, and had already gathered up all the stray screws and put them back in the box. Tabby marveled at how she hadn't had to tell him what to do next; they were obvious tasks, but she was used to having to micromanage every project with her ex and constantly keep him on track if she wanted his help at all.

It didn't feel like Logan was looking for any excuse to get out of the work.

"What's next, boss?"

"We're going for a short hike," Tabby said. "Out to the gate."

"Let me get Franzi," Logan said.

Franzi was playing in the mud at the end of the garden, just in sight through the open door.

"We're going on a little trip, kitten!" Logan said.

Franzi got very still and looked up at him cautiously. "Am I going away?"

Tabby busied herself putting the screw gun in the case while Logan crouched down and quietly reassured the little girl. As cute and charismatic as he was, it was his charm with Franzi that tested Tabby's resolve the most. But it didn't matter how good a stand-in dad he was being, she was absolutely not going to get involved with this disaster of a guy any more than she already regretted committing to.

"There's a ladder against the back of the house we'll need to take out with us," Tabby said briskly.

"Will you help me carry it, Franzi?"

Whatever Logan had said to her, it had set the little girl's fears to rest and Franzi jumped up eagerly.

She was much more of a hindrance to the job than a help, being barely more than three feet tall. She took the rungs between Tabby and Logan, who had to carry it lower than comfortable so she could think she was assisting, and she careened into it and tripped several times, nearly dragging them down.

But she was so cheerful about being a helper that Tabby couldn't begrudge her the extra effort. The sun was dipping towards the horizon, hidden behind the fringe of trees and ridges of the nearby hills, and the light was starting to fade. It was a pleasant evening, cool after a sweltering day, and gravel crunched beneath their feet.

"What fabulous act of strength can I perform next?" Logan asked, as they rounded the curve to the gate.

"It doesn't require any great strength," Tabby said, though it would have been a struggle getting the old-fashioned all-wood ladder this far by herself. "I'm just about four inches too short to do this job." She stopped them right at the gate and set up the ladder. "I've wanted that sign down for five years."

The ladder unfolded and Tabby held the far side as Logan climbed up to the very top. At least on the opposite side of the ladder, she wasn't staring up at his ass, even if she did get one brief, accidental look at his crotch as he went up.

Franzi called unnecessary instructions from the bottom

of the ladder. "A little FARTHER, Uncle LOGAN. Over that way!"

Logan pretended to be confused, reaching into space. "Over here?"

Franzi giggled. "No! The OTHER way!"

Logan had to stretch to actually reach the hanging sign, and stepped up on the step that undoubtedly would have been marked DON'T STAND HERE if the ladder hadn't been a hundred years old and made long before OSHA. The ladder swayed, and Tabby hung on for dear life. But the sign came off the hooks and Tabby was looking fixedly away when he came back down the ladder, telling herself that her heart was pounding because she'd worried for him crashing down and suing her for a broken arm, not for any other reason.

"This will be good for kindling," she said, taking the big sign from Logan with a grimace of dismay.

"Was Big Dawg your husband's name?"

Tabby shook her head. "It predated us. But really, *Big Dawg Dude Ranch*? It's worse than *Better Behave*."

"Not much is worse than *Better Behave*," Logan scoffed.

"I'm sure I could come up with something," Tabby teased.

They walked back, and Franzi was clearly tiring out, leaning against the ladder as they walked and not even pretending to help.

"I should get her to bed," Logan observed. "I'll try to get the stalls mucked after she's down."

Tabby already recognized that Logan was spreading himself thin. He got up as early as she did, and worked full days at the auto shop while Franzi was in day care, then came home to feed his niece and get her to bed. He always made himself available to help Tabby, but she could tell that it was a challenge to juggle an active little girl, a full time job, and still get anything else done. "Take the night off," she suggested. "Letisha will be here tomorrow morning to babysit Franzi and I need to make sure we're on the same wavelength for riding before I sign us up for a show."

Logan gave her one of his slow, teasing smiles and Tabby reminded herself that it wasn't serious. "Ready to go for a ride?"

"No! Yes! Don't say it like that! You are just a horse I bought." Tabby pinched the bridge of her nose. "Don't make this harder than it already is."

"Harder, you say?"

"I'm going to sell you to a stockyard," Tabby threatened, but she could not help but laugh. "Go get your girl to bed. I'll do the stalls and see you in the morning."

12

$\mathcal{I}$t was easy to forget that Logan was also a horse. Tabby suspected that it was a mental defense mechanism, that shifters simply didn't fit into her comfortable worldview, so she refused to think about it. Logan was a good-looking, down-on-his-luck charity case with an adorable little girl he was struggling to do right by. Better Behave was a dream-come-true horse that couldn't possibly measure up to Tabby's rosy memories.

The two lived separately in Tabby's brain and she was excited and nervous to get back on Better Behave.

And the name was going to have to go.

Tabby told herself that calling him Beauty would be too dangerous to Logan's ego, so she'd settled on Beau for his barn name. It was easier to think about what she would call him than it was to think about riding him again. Surely she had exaggerated how strong and graceful he was, and Tabby was wrestling with how weird it might be to ride Logan-the-person.

Letisha showed up promptly at nine, after Tabby had

done her morning chores in the barn, eaten breakfast, and watered the garden.

Tabby waved at her mother through the car window as Letisha bounced out. She'd been teaching Letisha for a year now, and the girl was reliable and a talented rider. She was just starting to shop for her own horse.

"Hi, Miss Tabby!" Letisha called.

Logan came down from the stable with Franzi as Tabby and Letisha exchanged friendly hugs and her mother drove away.

"I'm Logan," he said, and Letisha solemnly shook his hand. "This is Franzi."

Franzi tried to hide behind Logan.

"This is Letisha," Logan said, trying to coax Franzi around to meet her.

Letisha squatted down. "Hi, Franzi," she said kindly. "Do you like horses, too?"

"Not SUPOZE to be a horsey," Franzi muttered into the back of Logan's knees.

"She takes a little while to warm up to people," Logan said desperately. "Letisha is going to be your friend, Franzi."

"I'd like that, Franzi," Letisha said warmly. "I brought some books with me today. Do you like to read?"

Franzi looked reluctantly around Logan. "Uh-huh."

"Me, too." Letisha managed to make it sound like a state secret that she was sharing. "I have a book about a horse named Jewel and a cat named Wings. Have you ever heard of a cat with wings?"

"Amy has wings," Franzi offered shyly.

Letisha looked confused, but took it in stride. "Maybe we could read it together, if that sounds fun?"

Franzi gave her a long look from behind Logan and

then abruptly seemed to decide that Letisha was safe. Was it instinct, or just Letisha's easy air? "I'll show you my ROOM," Franzi declared.

Logan trailed after them as Franzi dragged Letisha by the hand up to their apartment.

Tabby busied herself in the barn, getting the tack she needed for Logan and adjusting her riding helmet unnecessarily.

By the time he came back down the stairs, she had half-convinced herself that this was all an elaborate scam, that shifters weren't a thing, that she'd hallucinated Franzi's shape-changing, and she was on the brink of a mental breakdown. Magic horses? Shapeshifting? It was all impossible. What was she even doing?

"You ready for this?" Logan asked gently.

"Not even a little," Tabby confessed. "And I'm dying to do this, at the same time. You've been here a whole week, and absolutely nothing magical has happened this entire time. I'm questioning my own sanity right now."

"You should be," Logan joked. "I mean, you've resisted my charms for a *whole week*. There *must* be something wrong with your head!"

"Ha ha," Tabby mock-laughed. "How much space do you need? Should we go outside? Do you need eye of newt or holy water? Will there be chanting?"

Logan laughed. "No, it's just a natural *shift*. This is plenty of space."

Knowing that he was the horse that she'd fallen in love with was one thing, but seeing him shift was something else entirely.

One moment, Logan was standing there with a rakish grin, tipping his hat in her direction, then he shimmered in place and seemed to *step out of himself* as a horse. A breathtaking horse, with that same white forelock that he had as a man.

"Where do your clothes go?" Tabby asked, reaching out to touch his gleaming neck without conscious direction. If he was beautiful as a man, and Tabby was willing to admit that he was, he was twice as gorgeous as a horse.

Better Behave—Beau—was everything she'd remembered and more. He was tall and every inch of him shone with strength and health. His coat was glossy and his eyes were bright as he lowered his nose to touch Tabby. She had to stroke that nose, absolutely as head-over-heels as she'd been the first time she met him, and reach up to run her fingers though that shocking white forelock.

"Is it really still you?" she asked, reminding herself that this was Logan and she probably shouldn't be caressing him so casually.

He gave a nicker and nodded his head.

Tabby made herself stop petting him and swallowed. "Okay, then. Let's see how you handle the course."

Setting the saddle on his back was one thing, fastening the girth was a little more awkward now that she knew there was a human man under the horseflesh. Tabby could just picture Logan's smirk and the joke he'd probably make as she tightened the girth. He took the bit gracefully and Tabby led him to the mounting block with her heart in her mouth.

She set her foot in the stirrup and swung into the saddle...and every shred of reservation she'd had simply vanished.

There were horses, and then there were *horses*, and Logan was absolutely the best animal she'd ever been up on. It wasn't just his conformation and strength, or his smooth gait as he stepped out. It was the way that Tabby had never been so in tune with a creature, or so utterly comfortable.

He followed the guidance of her knees and thighs before Tabby had even consciously realized she was telling him what she wanted, like they were connected at some higher level. The power between her legs was dizzying.

He walked sedately out of the barn and trotted to the course, pausing at the gate so Tabby could lean over and open it, and backing up so she could close it again. Then, like water, he was gliding forward and angling for the first jump.

Tabby had expanded the course since his first visit, but Logan needed no directions; she could simply ride and let Logan choose his stride as they struck out for the first jump. He sprang over the vertical jump, made simple work of the training cavaletti, and had so much extra length over the oxer that Tabby knew they'd have cleared any pool she'd ever jumped.

There was a triple bar for Tabby's more advanced students, and Logan sailed right over it with space to spare. He made his turns tight and neat, and Tabby only had to stay balanced in the saddle and flow with the motion. It was the most exhilarating course she had ever jumped, and she regretted not starting her stop watch.

Logan snorted but obeyed when Tabby slowed him to a halt. She couldn't resist leaning forward to stroke his neck. "You beautiful, terrible beast," she said in awe. "Let's do it again with a timer. Watch your step going into the in-and-out. You took off a little too close the last time."

Logan snorted and shook his head.

"Going to argue about it?" Tabby chided him. "Back to the start, big guy, and show me what you got. We're on the clock this time."

Logan took the course with the best time that any

horse had ever done for Tabby and she ended with an exhilarated laugh as Logan bounced in place.

"That was amazing, Miss Tabby!"

Tabby looked over her shoulder to find that Letisha was standing with Franzi at the gate and nudged Logan in their direction. Letisha was holding a dvd case and Franzi stared at them with big, amazed eyes.

"Not SUPOZE to be a horsey," Franzi whispered, though Tabby only knew what she was saying by experience; it was too quiet to actually hear her.

"You got a new horse!" Letisha exclaimed as they got close. "He's so beautiful! What's his name?"

"Lo—Beau!"

"Lobo?"

Logan lowered his head and let Letisha stroke his nose. Tabby told herself not to be jealous. "Beau. Just Beau," Tabby said sheepishly. She was awful at lying. "What did you need, Letisha?"

"I wanted to ask Mr. Logan if we could watch a movie that I brought." Letisha looked around expectantly.

Because, like an idiot, Tabby had told her that she would be working with Logan on the course.

"I...uh…" She was *really awful* at lying. Logan stepped sideways and huffed impatiently. Should Tabby try to dismount and distract Letisha so they could swap places? The theme for Benny Hill seemed to be running through her head. "He's...away for the moment, but I think that movie will be fine," she said awkwardly. It looked like a harmless kiddy movie to Tabby's untrained eyes.

Letisha didn't seem to notice her hesitation, thoroughly distracted with making googly eyes at Logan as she stroked his nose. "Okay," she said cheerfully. "Thanks, Miss Tabby!"

She took Franzi's hand and led her back to the barn. "Let's go watch the movie, Franzi!"

Tabby heaved a sigh of relief that was echoed by the horse between her legs. "Let's do the course a few more times, and then we'll go for a trail ride," she suggested. Logan nodded his head, the bright forelock waving between his ears.

13

*L*ogan was not sure that he'd ever experienced anything like having Tabby ride him.

He'd caught the tail-end of a few of her lessons and knew that she was a competent teacher. He'd seen her riding and lunging her boarders so he knew she was a skilled equestrian with obvious experience. Having her on his back was something else entirely.

She was a comfortable weight there, not any great burden, but a very definite presence. She rode him with a light rein, using only her legs for direction, and every one of her aids was sure and clear. Logan had been ridden by amateurs before and sometimes their intentions were muddy and confusing, even with human intelligence to interpret it. With Tabby, he didn't have a single moment of wondering what she wanted, and he was not only eager to meet her expectations, but aligned in desire.

They were a team, he thought. *This* was everything a horse and rider could be.

Everything…and more than he dared to hope for.

She was the whole package, Logan was completely

convinced. He'd met sexy women, smart women, and good riders, but they were rarely the same person. She was all of those things, and Logan had never met anyone as *genuine*.

They trained on the course for nearly an hour, Tabby adjusting the jumps and timing his strides.

Then, to his delight, Tabby took him out on the trail.

This was a considerably longer route than their first trip, when she still thought he was just a horse and he thought she was just a mark.

They trekked up a challenging trail, winding through forest, along the edges of neighboring farms, and into the hills. A straight stretch of packed path was the perfect place to test a flat-out gallop, and Logan anticipated the touch of Tabby's legs and settled into a ground-eating dash that he only reluctantly ended when the trail got rougher and Tabby eased him down to a ground-covering walk.

"Good job, Beau."

He could fly with her on his back, he thought, confident of her balance, and he was learning every quirk of her seat. They were so attuned to each other that they sighed with regret in unison when the ranch came back in sight.

Tabby took him back in through the gate and dismounted, patting him and praising him as if she'd forgotten he was Logan. "Who's a gorgeous horse? Who's a joy to ride?"

Logan shifted, and found Tabby's hand stroking his chest.

"Oh, my gosh, how do you do that?" Tabby asked breathlessly, snatching her hand back. "Where does the rest of you go? Will I get my saddle back? That's a custom Arion and I'm going to be pissed if it's lost in some shifter abyss somewhere."

Logan felt his mouth curve up in a smile. "I'll bring it back with me, promise."

She had to look up to meet his eyes, and Logan desperately wanted to bend down and kiss her. She was so pretty and lively, and she smelled like sweat and leather and...him. That was what was making him feel so possessive. It wasn't magical instinct, just animal instinct. He would react the same to anyone who had just spent a few hours making prolonged close contact.

It was actually hard not to touch her again now, and Tabby was fluttering her hands like she wasn't sure what to do with them. "That was...ah...great. You go over everything I put in front of you like it's not even there. I'll definitely get us set up for a show. I think there's one in Missoula next weekend. I wouldn't normally rush a horse into showing so soon, but you're...special. I mean, magical special. Ha ha. Wow. And if we don't get enough points this summer, we can't qualify for the Grand Prix in August. I mean, it's insane to even think about that. But the money would be so good and you'd be a shoo-in. If we could come up with the entry fee, of course. I've never met a horse like you. I mean, there clearly *isn't* another horse like you. You're not a horse. Except that you are..."

Logan figured that kissing her to make her stop talking would only result in getting slapped, but it was sorely tempting.

"Do you need to be...ah...brushed?" Tabby asked, putting her hands firmly behind her. She was adorably pink by this point, and Logan didn't think it was just sun. "Do you want some extra feed after that session? I'd normally toss in a few treats for that."

"I'm pretty hungry," Logan admitted, stretching. It had been a good workout. "I haven't thought about what I'm going to feed Franzi for dinner."

Tabby was looking fixedly to the side, like one of the buzzing flies had suddenly captured all of her attention and Logan resisted the impulse to flex and draw her awareness back to him. "I have some extra food in the crockpot I started this morning," she offered shyly without meeting his eyes. "You two could come over."

"I don't want to add to our debt," Logan said seriously, putting aside his stallion's urge to preen and show off for her. "You've already done so much for us."

"I'd like it," Tabby assured him, and her gaze flickered briefly to him. "It would be nice to have company, and I'd get sick of it before I got through the leftovers." She frowned thoughtfully. "You can make a salad, if you want, and fill up the dishwasher afterwards."

Logan tipped his hat at her. "It would be my pleasure," he said. "Let me go relieve the sitter. You said her mom would be here at five."

It was hard to resist the urge to walk backwards to keep his eyes on Tabby the whole way, and he had to remind himself that this was all just business.

Never mind that it felt like they'd just gone through a few hours of sweaty foreplay.

14

Tabby wasn't sure why she was so nervous about having her horse and his four-year-old ward over for dinner. She already knew all of his torrid secrets, between watching his niece turn into a foal and the research she'd dug up on him when she was trying to get her horse back.

She's already pressed herself wantonly against him and ridden him for several hours and…

Tabby yanked her thoughts back to Logan's human side.

On paper, he was a dirtbag, through and through. His records insisted that he was a con man with a shady past and a dozen misdemeanors, a lot of questionable history, and at least four separate identities.

In person, he was trying to gently redirect a four-year-old from touching every single thing in her house.

"This is a really pretty place you've got here," he said, looking around.

Tabby followed his gaze with pride. It did look good, with modern appliances paired tastefully with vintage restoration. "I did most of it myself," she admitted. "You want to destroy a good marriage? Try remodeling a house together." She regretted adding that as soon as the words were out of her mouth. What was wrong with her that she couldn't just say *thank you* like a normal person?

Logan gave her a smoldering look. "I don't think that working together destroys a good marriage, only a bad one. I've worked with you a little now, and you're a good partner."

Tabby opened her mouth but had absolutely no response for that.

Fortunately, Franzi tugged on Logan's arm until he bent down and she could stage whisper, "I have to go potty!"

"Down the hall on the left," Tabby said, pointing. "I'll set the table."

Franzi pulled Logan down the hall with her insistently, then slammed the door on him.

The timer went off while Tabby was still laying out plates and she went to take the tube biscuits out of the oven.

She came back with a basket of biscuits to find Logan setting the table. "Can I get drinks?" he offered, after the napkins were spread out at each place.

"Glasses are in the left cabinet. There's cold water in the fridge, ice in the freezer. Oh, I've got some milk. Do you want a beer?"

"Water's great for me. I'll pour Franzi some milk."

"Good, because I'm not actually sure I *have* any beer left. I think I drank the last one when my horse left me. I like ice in my water, please."

Franzi returned from the bathroom. "I flushed!" she announced.

"Did you wash your hands?" Logan asked her.

"I used soap!" Franzi said, which was apparently a yes, and when she spread her hands in proof, they were still coated in bubbles.

"Let's go finish rinsing those," Logan suggested, chasing her back down the hallway.

Tabby finished pouring the drinks herself, but Logan picked up where she left off when he came back, dropping ice cubes into her water without reminder.

She dished them each bowls of crock pot chicken stew. "How much will Franzi eat?"

"I'm hungry!" Franzi declared as she scrambled up onto a chair.

"We'll start with just a little," Logan countered. "You can get more," he promised her.

The chair was clearly too short for Franzi, and Tabby vowed not to worry about the food she managed to drop and to get a booster seat for future three-foot guests. One with a buckle, she decided, after Franzi had scrambled in and out of her chair a dozen times chasing dropped food, her napkin, her fork, her biscuit, and her shoe.

Logan shot her an apologetic look each time, and Tabby had to chuckle and shrug. It certainly took the pressure off of the meal, making Franzi the focus of their conversation by necessity. Tabby had been worried that it would be too date-like, and give Logan unreasonable expectations…and she'd been worried that she might *want* to live up to those expectations. But there was nothing romantic about Logan trying to chase stew off of Franzi's face every few minutes, or the little girl's lively and half-incomprehensible chatter.

They did manage a *little* grown-up talk when Franzi remembered to eat. Tabby told Logan more about her dreams for the ranch. "I've had several offers to sell the place. A lot of these farms and ranches near Nickel City are being bulldozed to build suburbia and this is apparently a sweet spot. Veronica Chase tried to buy it before we got it, and then she tried to snake it from Hank when the divorce was in process. Her office still sends me an offer every couple of months, but at this point, she's been such a —" Tabby glanced at Franzi, who was drinking her milk with hands so buttery from biscuits that she was surprised she had a grip on the glass. "Anyway, I'm not interested in selling."

"You shouldn't," Logan agreed. "This is an amazing place."

Logan had hair-raising tales about growing up with a circus. "Steven and I went to live with our grandparents when my mom skipped out." He eyed Franzi, who was spreading her napkin carefully in her lap again. "Dad started drinking, and it wasn't a great place to raise kids. Clancy stayed with the act longer than I did."

"That sounds awful," Tabby said quietly.

"You don't really notice it as a kid," Logan said. "You notice the music and the excitement, the cool animals and the noisy games. Cotton candy and corndogs, and a new place to explore every few weeks. You don't miss something you don't know you can have." He was still looking at Franzi, his mouth set in determination.

Tabby told herself that he had not gotten any hotter since the meal started.

Franzi was still eating her first serving, and slowing down drastically, when Tabby and Logan were finished. "I'll clear up," Logan volunteered. He froze halfway to standing. "I'd promised to make a salad," he remembered. "I'm so sorry!"

"That's fine," Tabby said. "You were a little busy, and there was enough of a meal without it."

Logan didn't look convinced as he gathered up their plates. "I still owe you," he said firmly.

"Well, then you'll have to come over again some night." Tabby rose to show him the trick to opening the dishwasher and how the insert of the crockpot came out to wash. "This was…really nice."

Logan shot a skeptical glance back out of the open kitchen door at Franzi, who was looking at her reflection in her dirty spoon and making faces. "You must be kidding."

"It was," Tabby insisted. "I would have had too many leftovers and gotten sick of stew, and it's nice to run the dishwasher after one meal instead of three without feeling wasteful. I liked having company." It came out more wistfully than she meant it to.

"It's the best meal I've had in yonkers," Logan said. He was standing unsettlingly close, and he had that flirty little smile on his face that Tabby kept telling herself not to take seriously.

"Who says *yonkers*?" Tabby teased breathlessly. "Is that a circus thing?"

"I have to go potty!" Franzi announced, starting to get down.

Logan sprang into action. "Wait, honey. Your hands are all dirty."

Over her strident protests, he wiped off her face and both hands, and dabbed at the stew on the front of her shirt before he released her to trip off down the hall.

"I'll clean this up," he promised, looking at the circle of disaster where Franzi had been sitting.

"Uncle LOGAN! My pants are STUCK!"

Tabby ended up loading the dishwasher and was cleaning up the splash radius around Franzi's chair when Logan returned.

"I have no idea how she managed to zip her shirt into her pants," he said. "Oh, let me do that."

He took the dishrag from Tabby and finished cleaning while Tabby ransacked her pantry for dessert. "I have some Girl Scout cookies," she announced, just as Franzi returned from her adventures in the bathroom.

"COOKIES!" Franzi said in delight, clambering back up into her chair.

Tabby realized that she should have asked Logan if dessert was a good idea. Franzi had already had a long exciting day and she wasn't sure if sugar on top of that was a recipe for disaster.

"You can have *one*," Logan said firmly.

Franzi watched with suspicious eyes as Tabby served one cookie to each of them. It would have been way too easy to eat the entire box, and Tabby thought this was another point in favor of having Logan and Franzi over for dinner again.

Franzi reduced her cookie to crumbs as she ate it, talking non-stop, and Tabby understood even less of what she said than before.

Logan insisted on sweeping, a task severely hampered by having to keep a constant eye on Franzi and tell her not to touch things as she careened around the house. Tabby held the dustpan for him.

"I've got to get her into bed before she collapses," Logan said regretfully, as Tabby dumped the crumbs.

"I'm not sweepy," Franzi said drunkenly. She yawned and didn't seem to recognize the irony, but Tabby and Logan chuckled. She didn't protest when Logan picked her up, and after she stretched to try to reach the ceiling, she snuggled down into his arms and lay her head on his shoulder.

"Thanks for dinner," he said, and Tabby thought his gaze was more intense than the moment deserved.

"You were great today," Tabby said. "I really appreciate your hard work."

"I had a great rider," Logan said.

Tabby watched them go, telling herself that the warmth she felt was flattery, not fondness.

15

____

Spring in the mountains of Montana came in with a vengeance, Logan realized. The growing season was short, but fierce, and Tabby warned Logan that the garden was absolutely all or nothing. The day that Logan moved in, the rows for carrots and potatoes were barely more than tiny sprouts. Within the week, they were ankle high and choked with opportunistic bindweed and chickweed. In a month, there was a jungle of unruly plants.

"Do you ever stop working?" Logan asked. Franzi was still asleep, and he had just a short window of opportunity before he had to get her up and take her into town.

"Did I wake you up feeding the horses? It's supposed to rain today," Tabby said, sitting back on her heels and wiping her hands on her pants. She wasn't wearing a hat, though Logan thought she should be; the back of her neck was already ruddy. Every so often while they were working, her collar would gap to show a distinct tan line and a tantalizing glimpse of comparatively pale skin. "I'd rather do it now than be all wet later."

"No comment," he said with a chuckle, when Tabby flushed the color of her sunburn.

He crouched down and began pulling up handfuls of weeds. "But this is supposed to be my job," he said apologetically.

"You've…kind of got your hands full," Tabby said as she moved to put the weed bucket in reach of both of them.

"I still mean to honor our agreement," Logan said seriously. "I'll get it all done somehow."

Every morning, he left with Franzi, often making several extra trips up the stable stairs for things they'd forgotten. He returned with her early each evening after a full day of work at the auto shop and tried to get work done with Tabby, but having a forty-pound shadow definitely complicated his productivity. The little girl might entertain herself for a while with mud pies while he helped Tabby hang sheetrock or install plumbing, but everything required frequent breaks because Franzi got hungry, thirsty, bored, or had to be accompanied to the bathroom. Meals, without exception, took twice as long as Logan expected.

He mucked out and bedded the stalls one at a time while Franzi played in the fresh hay. She didn't offer to shift, and when Logan suggested it from time to time, she shook her head. "Not supoze to be a horsey," she would mumble. Then she would ask for a snack and Logan would put his tools away and make her one.

After he got her down to sleep at night, Logan would show up to do some of the other tasks that Tabby had assigned him. The horses took a lot of work, and finishing the bunkhouses in whatever time they could carve out was a slow, laborious process. Tabby was up as late as he was every night, and awake in the morning even earlier.

"Out of curiosity, how did you get past the barn security system? That's a state-of-the-art keypad setup."

"I've got a keypad cracker," Logan said.

"That sounds very James Bond," Tabby chuckled.

"Oh, it is. Pocket-sized, and it shifts right along with me."

"How many times were you sold before I had the dumb luck to get you?"

Logan tossed a fistful of chickweed into the bucket between them. "A few dozen, maybe? It's not something we could do too many times, no matter how many different identities Clancy had. The reason we picked you, actually, is that we'd pissed off a pretty important guy with deep pockets and the heat was on; we were looking for someone that would be off the radar. Before you, it was rodeo owners and big name horse brokers. But Clancy wanted to keep a low profile for a while, and your wanted post was just our speed."

"Oh, thank you," Tabby said tartly. "I'm so glad I have *rube* written all over my forehead. That's what every woman wants to hear."

"You're not a complete rube," Logan teased. "Though I gotta say, I really question your character judgment! You should vet your renters more carefully."

Tabby laughed, the way he meant her to. "It was an impulsive choice, but I'm not regretting it…yet." She moved further away and Logan concentrated on the next row of plants until their work brought them together again. Weeding was trickier than it sounded, especially when the interlopers were nearly the same size as the seedlings. Franzi, in an early attempt to help, had ripped up several feet of fragile plants. Logan had replanted them the best he could, but they still looked deeply traumatized and stunted.

"You aren't still feeling bad about those, are you? I haven't given up on them yet."

Tabby was carrying the full weed bucket to dump it in the compost bin, and Logan realized that he was staring at the wilted plants thinking mournfully of Franzi. She'd been ripped away from her family and safety. Was she young enough to be resilient, or would losing her parents stunt her forever? How could Logan possibly be the family she needed? The scope of his responsibility was daunting.

"I was just thinking about Franzi," Logan said brusquely, standing to put a final handful of weeds in her bucket.

"Did you find out what happened to your brother?" Tabby asked gently.

"Car accident. An inexperienced driver took a left turn across traffic. Franzi was in the back seat and was barely scraped up in her car seat, but both her parents and the other driver died."

"Thank God for car seats," Tabby murmured. "How's she doing?"

"She's amazing," Logan said without hesitation. "She loves it here, she loves the day care, and I don't know how to thank you for letting us stay here." He hadn't realized how close he was standing, or how his voice had automatically dropped.

She frowned and pushed a loose lock of hair behind her ear while she looked fixedly at his forehead. "Tomorrow's show will be the real test of how well this will work out," she warned him. "I told you this wasn't charity, and I'm not interested in your alternate payments. I needed a solid show horse, and that's what you're going to be."

Logan didn't want her to think he was just flirting with her, or and he certainly didn't want to jeopardize their working relationship, even if she was really hot. But he couldn't resist grinning at her. "You'll come around on those alternatives."

"Check your ego, cowboy," Tabby sniffed. "And bring your A game to Missoula tomorrow morning, because I expect to get my money's worth out of you."

Logan tipped his hat to her. "Yes, ma'am," he agreed. He couldn't resist adding a wink.

s sure as Tabby had tried to pretend she was, she was not convinced that she and Logan could take the Missoula show until they got there.

It was a small, mostly-local competition, and just a one-day affair. Letisha was amenable to taking Franzi for the full day, but there was an awkward dance between Logan and Beau as he had to juggle giving Letisha last-minute human instructions and then shifting to be loaded into the trailer as a horse. Pulling out with an empty trailer was too much of a risk, in case Letisha was watching from the apartment window or someone else noticed at the fairgrounds when they arrived.

"Is that as boring a ride as I think it is?" Tabby asked as she guided Logan from the trailer.

He nodded and sighed.

"Maybe you can ride in the cab with me on the way home," Tabby suggested. "It can be your reward for winning, if you do."

Logan snorted a laugh at her and nuzzled her hair.

Tabby told herself it wasn't an intimate action; horses did that all the time. No one would think it was weird.

They jumped the course without any faults, and riding Logan in public was even more fun than riding him privately. He was showy beneath her, but focused on their craft, and they very casually swept the competition. Logan didn't even break a sweat, and Tabby had never felt so at home in a saddle.

Tabby accepted the championship ribbon and check with a feeling of dizzy relief and minor guilt.

It hadn't been a terrible mistake to do this. Logan had kept his end up and Tabby knew she'd ridden well and showed him off in style. Their jumps were perfect and their teamwork was flawless.

Tabby thought that she might have won on a lesser horse; the competition was not that steep, and the course didn't seem that challenging. She led Logan off the field.

He pranced and arched his neck and did fancy dressage steps back to the barn for his rubdown.

"We did it," Tabby said in wonder as she took off the tack and stashed it in the trailer.

Logan's head bobbed up and down in agreement and he stomped proudly.

"This can't last forever," Tabby said regretfully. When she heard the words out loud, she wasn't sure if she was talking about competing with Logan or that giddy falling-in-love feeling she was wrestling to suppress.

Logan pressed his big nose into her arms and Tabby reached up to comb her fingers through the white streak in his forelock.

Neither one was forever.

Logan couldn't pretend to be her horse for very long. How did lifespans work for a shifter horse? Jumpers rarely showed for more than ten years because it was hard on the joints and a compassionate rider put their mount's health before winning prizes indefinitely.

And romance?

Tabby wasn't good at romance, proven by her own track record of divorce and disaster. The curious, magical connection she felt with Logan was all in her head, fleeting and just out of reach. If she was falling in love, it was a terrible mistake, and she'd be left with nothing but regret. Logan was a *con man*. Tabby knew his record, and she'd read the reports of the women he'd loved and left wanting. Maybe Franzi had some claim on his affections, but Tabby knew that his true heart was carefully guarded. He was a playboy, a heedless flirt, and she had no one to blame but herself if she ignored all his warning signs.

When he was a horse, it was easy to love him without reservation. He was beautiful and graceful. He carried her so lightly that Tabby felt like a Mongol warrior or an Amazon princess, powerful and unstoppable. They were so in tune that it almost hurt.

But it was just a horse and the girl who loved him.

It all went away when he was a man and she was a woman.

Oh, his glances were full of fire and lust, but Tabby knew a bad idea when it smacked her in the face. And Logan Kennedy was a *bad idea.*

She pushed his velvet-soft nose away. "I'm just doing this until we're established," she warned him. "To the Grand Prix this fall at the most." If they could do enough shows to get the points and save for the entry fee, winning the Grand Prix would solve all of her money woes.

Logan nodded, but pressed his face back at her and Tabby could not resist petting his nose and neck.

"You did great," she murmured. "So good."

For a long moment, she just stroked him like that, soaking in their triumph.

Did it matter that they'd never be closer than this? Why would she long for anything more?

ittle girls took a lot of money, Logan learned quickly.

She didn't eat that much, but Logan was appalled by how much her cute little clothes cost, and he had to curb his impulse to buy her every toy she looked wistfully at. The food she liked best was fortunately not the most expensive, but Logan wanted her to eat healthy food and he was still unsure how much better organic noodles and butter were than their cheaper competition. Since he was ferrying a four-year-old, Logan sprang for car insurance, and gas was more than he ever remembered paying.

Tiny Paws was a huge chunk of change, on top of that.

The auto shop job was still at minimum wage, which was frightfully small after benefits were deducted, and when he started an official mentorship, there would be union dues owed monthly, even though Logan was confident that it would be a good long-term tradeoff. He and Mason got along well, and he was starting to count the rest of the staff as his *friends.* Many of the shifters that he ran into regularly at the grocery store or day care drop off would pause to chat, and he felt like he was part of a community. He and Tabby agreed to split any prize money they made, but the payouts were minor so far, although they were racking up the qualifications for the big show and a decent pot in August.

Logan wasn't sure what he'd be doing if it hadn't been for Tabby. Still living in Billings, undoubtedly, with no prospects or opportunity. The idea of raising Franzi in that horrid apartment was appalling, and if he was busier than he'd ever been in his life, he was also happier.

Tabby gave him no slack, and pretended her kindness was cutthroat, even though she clearly didn't know the meaning of the word.

Aside from training and doing any minor jump shows that didn't require overnight travel, they worked together on the ranch in the evenings, Franzi in tow, and they ate most dinners together. Logan insisted on helping in the kitchen and cleaned up afterwards, as much as Franzi let him, and he brought contributions when he could. The garden started putting out fresh greens and promises of fruit with little flowers. Logan learned more about plants than he ever imagined would be interesting. A make-shift playset just beside the garden began to take shape, starting from a pile of old tires that Logan pressure-washed, and a few sanded planks.

Franzi was playing on it one night after dinner, and Logan had the front wheel of Tabby's truck off to fix a slow leak in the tire.

"Not a lot of life left in these tires," he said regretfully, once he'd found the leak and patched it. "You'll want something better when there's snow on the roads."

"I just need them to hold it together until I can get a few more boarders signed up," Tabby said, wiping off her hands. She was painting the porch in the dying light, and had just set up a bank of work lights so she could go a little longer. Logan was not sure she ever stopped moving, and he was not sure he wanted her to. She was so fun to watch, with all her strength and energy. He wasn't sure how she was so sexy without trying.

Logan made sure that Franzi was staying safely out of the way and hefted the tire back into place, tightening down the lugs and lowering the lift.

Then, because Franzi was still very involved in her imaginary play and it was only early evening, Logan picked up a paintbrush and went to help Tabby. The porch had a lot of fancy decorative posts that took careful brush strokes to fill correctly and Logan had already spent a fair amount of time hand-sanding them.

The porch was one of the prettiest features from the outside, wrapping around three sides of the old house, and it was undoubtedly an attempt at some kind of architectural style that Logan didn't know the name of. The rest of the house was a pretty standard two story farmhouse with aging siding and small, sensible windows with double panes of glass. It was going to look a lot better with fresh paint, and Tabby had consulted Logan about colors before deciding on a pure white with slate blue trim to match the original slate roof. Already, it looked considerably better than it had the first time Logan drove up in the rickety stock trailer.

Franzi fell asleep on the porch swing while they were putting the final touches on, and Logan let her slumber as he and Tabby went out into the driveway to admire as much as they could in the last daylight.

"It looks gorgeous," Tabby said, her voice full of pride.

"Yeah." Logan wasn't looking at the house, but at Tabby, the planes of her face catching the final glow of sunset. The halo of the hair escaping her brown braid was golden in the low light.

"Veronica Chase can suck on an egg," Tabby said tartly. "I could not believe what she offered me the last time she tried to buy it."

"Tell her you already have a buyer. She'll offer twice as much."

Tabby glanced at him. "What, did you do real estate scams, too?"

Logan chuckled sheepishly. "Might have, once or twice."

"I'm not good at lying," Tabby said with a shrug.

"I would never have guessed!" Logan said in mock astonishment.

She elbowed him in the side and Logan realized that they were standing much closer together than he meant to be. He genuinely intended to respect their professional arrangement, but it was so natural to flirt with her and sidle up close...and sometimes, like now, he wanted nothing more than to lean over and kiss her, just to see if she would let him.

And if she let him kiss her...

"Will you teach me?" Tabby moved away to start coiling up the power cord that had plugged in the work light. She never stayed still for long.

Kissing? Logan struggled to remember what they were talking about. "Lying?" He trailed after her.

"You're incredibly good at it, according to Garrett, my investigator."

"Well, yes," Logan said modestly. "The first thing you do is remember that they don't *know* you're lying."

Tabby's face scrunched up in confusion. "What?"

"The only thing they know is what you tell them and what you show them. You might feel all guilty inside and know better, but they *don't*. Remembering that helps you bluff through."

"Should I be taking notes?"

"Don't write anything down," Logan cautioned. "No evidence. You can always backpedal on something you said and insist that the other person heard it wrong, but it's harder when it's in writing."

"Makes sense," Tabby said, nodding. "What else?"

"Direct their attention where you want it instead of waiting for it to go somewhere you don't want it," Logan said, pointing to a knot that Tabby was starting to roll up. While she was distracted juggling her coil and finding the end to pull through the loop, he slipped her phone from her back pocket and switched it with his own.

"So distract them?" Tabby said.

"Not just random distraction," Logan expanded, helping her find the loose end of the cord. "People know what they want, and a big part of staying ahead of them is understanding what that is and giving them just enough of their desire to keep them hooked."

Tabby slung the coiled cord onto the hook by the porch.

Standing well back, with absolutely no contact between them, Logan made a show of pulling the phone from his pocket.

"That's mine!" Tabby said, reaching back for hers and pulling out his. "When did you do that?"

"A magician never reveals his secrets."

Tabby swapped phones with him. "I supposed you'll pull a coin out from behind my ear next?"

Logan tucked some of her loose hair behind it, instead. "You're rich enough without it."

Tabby looked taken aback by the intimate gesture. "Not to hear Veronica Chase talk," she stammered, drawing away. "Can you believe she sent me another offer? It was another thinly-veiled threat that she'd get it when the property went into foreclosure anyway."

"I haven't even met her and I already hate her," Logan observed casually. It was probably a good thing he hadn't tried to kiss her. He didn't want to disrupt the careful balance that they had. "I should get Franzi into bed." He stepped back and touched the brim of his hat. "Goodnight."

"Goodnight," she echoed.

Franzi woke up as Logan was carrying her upstairs to bed. "It's dark out!" she observed in surprise.

"Time for sleeping," Logan told her, opening the door to his apartment with one hand. He didn't have to lock up, out here, and he was glad he wasn't having to juggle keys, too.

"Okay," Franzi said, putting her head back down on his shoulder.

He got her through her nighttime routine with less fuss than usual and stood for a while looking out of the kitchen window at Tabby's house.

He didn't want to mess up what they had, but he found himself yearning for something more.

Herd, his stallion said with a yawn.

Logan shook his head decisively. He couldn't let his libido risk his place here. Relationships were messy and unnecessary, and he was already knees-deep in commitment to a four-year-old filly shifter.

18

One night, halfway through the summer, Franzi's favorite word suddenly became *no*.

It was as if a switch had been flipped.

She went from a quiet, docile little thing with occasional streaks of stubbornness straight to an object of intense resistance.

The fried rice that she'd liked so much the night before was *icky*. She wouldn't eat it, or anything else except for the plain noodles that Logan finally broke down and made for her. The nightgown was *itchy*. Her stuffies were *stupid*. She wasn't going to go to bed and Uncle Logan *couldn't make her*.

Logan had run a lot of cons in his life, and he considered himself plenty good at getting people to do things for him. He had a cute-but-clueless act that could charm cash out of housewives at any grocery store or gas station. He'd talked his way out of more speeding tickets than he had any right to, and he could knock down a fight in a bar or start one with just a few well-chosen words, depending on how much chaos he felt like causing.

Even Clancy had been impressed by his wounded bird

performance as a horse. (They'd pulled more than one hit-and-run set up.)

And Franzi completely flummoxed him.

She wouldn't accept logic. She wouldn't succumb to charm. She had no interest in his bribery.

She was simply not going to bed and when Logan tried to take her by the hand and forcibly put her there, she dropped like a stone to the floor and began screaming her head off.

Logan had no idea what to do.

"Franzi, honey, we have to go to bed. It's time for sleeping."

"NO! I WON'T GO! YOU'RE MEAN! I'M NOT SWEEPY!"

She even nailed him with the dreaded, "YOU'RE NOT MY DADDY!" and cried piteously and then screamed and kicked when Logan tried to pick her up and give her a hug.

"I know you're having big feelings," Logan said desperately, trying to dredge up anything helpful from the hundreds of contradictory webpages he'd been reading. His brain felt broken. The pitch of her voice was like mental razor wire.

"NO! YOU'RE A MEANIE! I HATE YOU!"

Every word was like a dagger to his chest and Logan tried to sort out how words with no more than two syllables apiece could have that many barbs.

"Franzi, honey…"

"NO! DON'T TOUCH ME!"

Logan tried singing the lullaby that had worked with her the first time and she screamed so loud he couldn't hear his own words.

He shouted at her, "YOU HAVE TO GO TO BED!"

and she only shouted back louder, "NO! I WON'T GO TO BED!"

He couldn't just force her to do it, and every time that Logan had a glimpse of the frustration behind her fit, she would double down on her fury. "YOU DON'T CARE ABOUT ME!" Sometimes it fell away into nonsense words. "BLUE DOER ABLE MONEY!"

It went on until her voice was hoarse and Logan felt half-deaf.

Finally, desperate for a break, he went into his own room and sat down on his bed to stare sightlessly at the floor. Was *this* what being a parent was like? How did anyone *do* it?

Her shrieking stopped and Logan went out to find her fast asleep in the middle of the floor, boneless like a doll with her hands still in angry fists.

Logan left her there, tiptoeing carefully around to the little kitchen to take the whiskey out of the tall cabinet over the fridge.

He put it back without drinking any. He couldn't risk losing what was left of his shattered senses. If he had to drive her to a doctor…Logan suddenly wondered if he could even *take* her to a doctor if she got hurt. He didn't know anything about shifter kids. He didn't know anything about *kids*. Every time child services called to check in, he felt a stab of panic and unworthiness.

As much as he dreaded waking her, Logan couldn't leave her to sleep on the floor, so he gathered her up into his arms and took her to her bed. He tucked her in wearing all her clothes and unclenched her little fingers one at a time. She barely stirred as he pulled the covers up to her chin, only scrunched her eyes shut tighter and murmured a little as she snuggled down.

Logan turned on her nightlight and shut the door, then

went to his room to spend a long, sleepless night wondering if he'd done anything in his life *right*.

He must have finally fallen asleep, because he woke when Franzi crept into his bed with a giggle. "I swept in my clothes!" she exclaimed, with no hint of her previous night's anger or upset.

Logan wrapped an arm around her and kissed her curly head, but she had no interest in snuggling and quickly squirmed out of his embrace. "I'm hungry," she said sweetly.

"Do you want fried rice?" Logan asked trepidatiously. He was out of noodles and waffles.

"I love fried rice!" Franzi said happily, and she turned to skip out of the room.

Four year olds were insane.

That's all there was to it.

She ate twice as much as she usually did and Logan wondered if this was what was hailed on the internet as a growth spurt. She didn't look any taller. Logan drank an entire pot of coffee and packed her bag for Tiny Paws.

He knew it was too good to be true when he told her to put on her shoes and she looked him in the eyes and said, "NO. I DON'T LIKE SHOES."

Logan wasn't about to argue his way through another fit and be late to work, so he just stuffed her shoes in her bag. Then he stooped and picked her up to football-carry her down the stairs and out to the truck. She giggled the whole way and let him buckle her into the car seat.

Other than her shoe-less feet, it was a normal drive to day care, and Logan simply carried her into Tiny Paws and set her down inside to scamper along the narrow entryway. "Is Tara here?" she called, clambering up over the baby gate.

Logan signed her in with Addison and then sank down to the miniature-scale bench to bury his head in his hands.

"You must be Franzi's dad."

There was a woman wearing a nurse's smock sitting on the far side of the door nursing a baby. Logan hadn't noticed them on his way in; she wasn't a shifter. Her dark-haired baby was sucking eagerly at one bare breast and Logan decided that if she wasn't embarrassed about it, he wouldn't be either.

"Uncle," he said hoarsely. "Guardian." Was it all settled? Logan was still expecting child services to swoop in and declare him unfit at any moment. Mrs. Gravis had visited Tabby's ranch a few times and seemed satisfied with his efforts, but after last night, he certainly *felt* unfit. "I guess." He mustered his manners. "I'm Logan Kennedy, ma'am."

"I'm Tara's mom, Vivian." She didn't have a hand free to shake, but she gave him a lift of her chin that Logan returned with a nod. "This bottomless pit is Shane. I'm guessing you had a tough morning."

"She yelled at me for an hour last night," Logan admitted. "And this morning she refused to wear shoes."

Vivian's smile was understanding. "They like to test their boundaries."

"I didn't even know she *knew* the word no," Logan said. "I think she's been softening me up."

"You haven't had her long?"

Logan did the math in his head. "Three weeks last Friday."

"Oh, she's starting to trust you. That's probably what this was about."

Logan stared at her. "That's trust? Screaming that she hates me is *trust?*"

Vivian fixed him with a direct look that was layered in

understanding. "Kids are complicated and contradictory. But if you haven't had her that long, she's probably just getting to the point where she's testing to see if you'll still keep her if she's bad or things go wrong. Was she in foster care?"

"Two years," Logan said, riddled with guilt. "I *didn't know*."

Vivian's smile was kind, with a flash of grief. "That was probably really hard, but you'd be amazed how resilient kids are. Tara lost her dad when she wasn't much older."

"Oh, I'm sorry," Logan said automatically. He eyed the baby, trying to figure out how the math worked before he decided it didn't matter.

"Thank you," Vivian said simply. "I'm sorry for your loss, also."

Logan started to protest that there hadn't been any loss, then snapped his mouth shut.

He'd lost a brother.

It didn't matter that they'd been estranged, or that Logan had been the one that had driven him away with his questionable morals and career choices. He was never going to see Steven again or have a chance to make things right with him. The abrupt addition of his brother's daughter to his life had been more important at the moment than taking the time to mourn, but it didn't mean that Logan didn't have his own complicated feelings to work through.

The baby popped off the nipple he'd been nursing and turned his head to stare at Logan curiously.

"All done?" Vivian covered herself up briskly and the baby gave a wail of outrage at having his meal removed, then allowed her to distract him with a jingling toy that he pulled into his mouth and grinned toothlessly around.

"We should get the girls together for a playdate sometime," Vivian offered, as she stood up and bounced Shane into her arms.

"Tara would be welcome out at our place," Logan offered, sure that Tabby wouldn't mind. "It's about five miles out of town at a ranch and she could come out for the day. We work most weekends, but maybe the Fourth? Tiny Paws is closed and I have the day off from my other job." He stood as well, out of courtesy, and also because he needed to get to said job.

"Oh, would you mind taking Tara? That would be amazing! I have to work and I wasn't sure what I was going to do with Tara all day. I can take Shane with me, but Tara gets so bored at the clinic."

That reminded Logan. "The clinic…is it a safe place to bring a…ah…?" She wasn't a shifter, and instinct wasn't giving him a single twinge of warning about her, but Logan had a lot of ingrained caution on the topic.

Vivian smiled at him as he trailed off. "There's a pediatrician at the clinic who's a shifter. My…ah…Doctor Becket. He'd be happy to see Franzi with any concerns you might have." She flushed a little and Logan guessed that her doctor was more than just a coworker. He had to wonder at the ethical implications of a relationship with her boss.

*You're in love with **your** boss*, his stallion snorted at him.

Tabby isn't my boss, Logan retorted. *And I'm not in love with her.*

But the idea arrested him. She was so smart and beautiful, and Logan couldn't ignore the way his heart always gave a little hiccup whenever he first saw her. He wanted to pretend that it was just a physical reaction to an attractive woman, but it was hard to deny that it felt like something more. He wanted to bask in Tabby's presence, not just nail her and not see her again.

Not *my boss,* Logan repeated, as much to himself as to his stallion. More importantly: **Not** *in love.* "Let's plan on the Fourth," he said firmly. "I'll give you the address and my phone number. It's a safe place for a pair of fillies to run around if you're okay with that."

"Not just a filly…" Vivian warned carefully.

A *unicorn.* It still seemed impossible. "It's a very private ranch," Logan promised.

"That sounds amazing. It was great to meet you, Mr. Kennedy."

"Logan is fine, ma'am," he said warmly.

"I'll call you Logan if you never call me ma'am again."

"Yes, ah, *Vivian.*" Some habits were hard to break.

Logan went to the auto shop with a lighter heart and set to work. Halfway through the day, he got a call from an unknown number. He stared at it suspiciously for a moment, then answered. It probably wasn't child services because Mrs. Gravis was in his contacts, but he couldn't take the chance of ignoring it. "Logan Kennedy."

"You're using your real name now, cousin?" Clancy's voice froze every ounce of relief out of Logan's chest.

"What do you want?" Logan asked cautiously as he wiped his hands on a rag and went outside. Mason shot him a look as he went, but nodded in understanding.

"It's not what *I* want," Clancy said with dangerous charm. "It's who wants *you.* Can we talk?"

This was how it always went. Logan and Clancy would split ways and just when Logan hit his most desperate, Clancy would be back with some foolproof plan that he couldn't say no to. It was always reasonable, and Logan was always weak enough to say yes.

"I've got a job now," Logan said. A minimum wage job, to be fair. "And Steven's little girl. I'm not running any more cons."

"Steven has a kid?" Clancy sounded skeptical.

"Had," Logan said flatly. "He and his wife died in a car accident. Franzi's mine now, and I'm not going to screw this up." He wasn't going to screw any of it up.

Clancy was quiet. "Is she a shifter?"

"Yeah," Logan said reluctantly, then wished he hadn't, suddenly struck with worry. Surely Clancy wouldn't think he had some claim on her. What would he want with a little kid? But Logan had been a little kid when he and Clancy were first running cons, and he could think of a dozen ways that Clancy might try to use an adorable, innocent shifter kid like Franzi. "I'm not interested in any more deals," he said firmly. "I don't do that anymore."

"You've gone soft," Clancy said with a knowing chuckle. "But give me some credit. I know how you feel, and I'm not going to ask you to do anything technically illegal. Straight sale, no funny business. All I'd ask is a perfectly reasonable agent fee for finding him. He's just your type, too, a total douchebag who deserves to be done dirty."

Logan felt his resolve waver. As hard as he was working, it sometimes felt like he was poorer than ever. His meager savings had melted away in the face of car insurance and the price of gas and a daily commute and day care. Somehow, his food bill had doubled, even though he knew that Franzi didn't eat nearly as much as he did and he ate several meals a week with Tabby. He wasn't sure how he was going to make the next month's day care bill in advance. And he was keenly aware that Tabby was scraping the bottom of her own barrel; he couldn't possibly ask her for anything more than she'd already given him.

He's not our herd, his stallion sniffed. *We drove him out.* But he didn't understand money, or debt, or the fact that child services might take Franzi if he couldn't support them.

The animal was convinced that everything was going to be fine and was sure that they would weather any complication.

"No, I'm done," Logan said firmly, wishing he was as confident as he sounded.

There was a slice of silence and Logan thought that Clancy had hung up until he spoke again. "I saw you tearing up the little local weekend shows with your lady friend," he said, so mildly that the hair on the back of Logan's neck stood up in warning. "Shame you two aren't going to the Grand Prix in Billings this year. You qualified."

Logan and Tabby had talked about that show, but she had shaken her head at the entry fee, despite the wistful look in her eye. "Takes money to make money," Logan said shortly, quoting Clancy's own words back at him.

"I could get you in, even cover the fee. My buyer is in that area anyway, and I'm sure he'd pay more for a prize winner."

"Why do you want me to do this so bad?" Logan asked suspiciously.

"The heat has been on," Clancy said frankly. "Your girlfriend is starting to be known in horse circles and she's got social credit I don't right now. She makes this sale, no one is sniffing the papers while they're being signed. I don't even have to come up with those papers, she's still got them from our previous sale."

"Leave Tabby out of this," Logan growled.

"She doesn't have to do anything but ride you," Clancy said, and it sounded dirty in his voice. "Are you, by the way? Riding her?"

"It's none of your business."

Clancy laughed. "The offer won't be on the table very long, cousin, and I'm guessing you don't have any better opportunities. Call me back at this number while it still works."

Logan hung up without answering and then regretted it.

Would it be so terrible to do one final grift?

He wanted to be a better person than he was. Tabby made him want to be that better person, and he was desperate to be a good dad for Franzi.

But the *right thing* didn't pay bills, and Clancy wasn't wrong. Logan didn't have a lot of options. He stared at his phone, and finally dialed it. "I need more information."

Wrong, his horse complained, but Logan was used to ignoring his instincts when it came to Clancy.

19

Tabby wasn't exaggerating how much she loved having Logan and Franzi over for dinner most nights. Cooking for herself was basically drudgery, but cooking for people who were enthusiastic about it was actively rewarding, and she was grateful to have a reason to pause after caring for the horses instead of diving into the next job with whatever leftovers she had in one hand.

"Whoa," Logan said as he and Franzi came in the kitchen door. "You're actually sitting down when it's not for a meal."

"Whoa!" Franzi said, pretend-galloping around the dining room table. "WHOA!"

Tabby had her computer open in front of her. "Trying to decide which bills to pay this month," she said bitterly. She and Logan had been doing well at all the shows they had managed to make, but the ones nearby were small and had mostly the same clientele, so the boost to her business hadn't been what she hoped it would be.

"You've got two new boarders for training," Logan

said, taking a seat opposite from her. "And more lessons than you had this spring."

"I lost a boarder, too," Tabby pointed out. Oreo's owner had reluctantly relocated to Oregon, and she hadn't had the heart to penalize him for breaking their contract.

Franzi was on her third lap of the table already, neighing enthusiastically. "Is it...that bad?" Logan asked cautiously.

Tabby sighed. "Last summer, the well got clouded and I had to redrill it and buy a new pump and pressure system. I did it on credit, and they're threatening to send the bill to collections on the final installment. Paying it off means skipping the mortgage this month, or selling the truck. I need the truck."

"What about the rentals?" Logan asked, frowning.

"Whoa!" Franzi said, as Logan caught her by the waist and turned her around.

"Run the other way so you don't get too dizzy," he advised.

Franzi happily trotted in the other direction, already reeling.

"That seems like good life advice," Tabby said wryly. "The rooms are nearly finished, but where do I get the money for the appliances and furniture? No one is going to rent an empty box, no matter how good the view is." She closed the laptop carefully. "I know that we're going the right direction, but this business is a slow build, and I don't have the *margin* to get through the tight spots. Maybe Veronica Chase *will* get her wish and scoop up the ranch for a song when I have to foreclose." She hadn't meant to say so much and hoped that Logan wouldn't pity her. "Anyway, I guess you should know. So you can be shopping for another place for you and Franzi, just in case." She sucked in a breath. "I've got a casserole in the oven. It should be ready in about twenty minutes. Can you help me make a salad to go with the hot dish?"

"All the food groups," Logan said, standing. "Meat, starch, vegetables, and ranch dressing."

"Ranch DRESSES!" Franzi said breathlessly.

She continued to make circles of the room as Logan followed Tabby into the kitchen. To her surprise, he didn't go to the cabinet to get the cutting board; one of the things she liked best about his help is that he didn't wait for her to tell him every detail about what needed done.

Instead, he closed the kitchen door.

"What's up?" Tabby said suspiciously as she stood up with the crisper and closed the fridge. He wasn't going to make a move on her in her kitchen, was he? She didn't want him to, did she? She put the vegetables on the island between them.

"I have an…opportunity."

"I'll need some more information than that," Tabby said tartly. Logan's discomfort was obvious. Clearly, he did pity her.

"Clancy called me today."

"Clancy Kennedy who sold me a horse in exchange for my life savings?" Tabby clarified. "Which vanished the first night, leaving me high and dry?"

"That Clancy, yes," Logan said, even more reluctantly.

"Has he got another scam for you?"

"Con," Logan corrected. "It's a con, not a scam."

"I'm sure there is a reason for that distinction," Tabby said. "I notice that this started as an *opportunity*, and we've moved into shadier territory pretty quickly."

"It's not *technically* illegal."

"Look, I'm listening, but you'd better spit out the details before I have to wring them out of you with a cheese grater."

"He wants to sell me again."

"*I* own you," Tabby said with a great deal more vinegar than she intended. It wasn't like she had any *actual* claim on Logan.

"I wouldn't do this without your okay," Logan said immediately. "And I told Clancy you had to buy in, and I didn't agree to do it yet. We *all* have to win."

"Except the poor sap who buys you. Let me tell you what *that's* like."

"He's a douchebag of the highest degree," Logan promised. "He's a predator of horse-crazy girls and he has more money than the Pope so he gets out of every accusation. He's a slum lord and cheats on taxes with fake charities. He's even a *bad rider*."

"And Clancy wants to *sell* you to him? What's the catch? Why do you even need me?"

He was quiet for a long moment, and didn't answer the question. "We have to enter the Grand Prix in Billings."

Tabby stared at him, wrestling with her misgivings and, even more, with the sheer desire that rushed through her.

The Grand Prix had big cash prizes—big enough to pay off both of her looming bills and furnish at least one of the rentals if they got the top ribbon.

Even better, the event was the highlight of the Montana jumper circuit. If she made a good showing with Logan, there was a good chance she'd pick up enough new students and training clients to keep the ranch going on its own.

And best yet, she'd be proving something to herself. That she really *was* a good rider, a good trainer, a good *person*—all things she had doubted since her divorce. She had what it took to get the blue ribbons. Winning the Grand Prix had been her dream when she bought Logan from Clancy in the first place.

But…

"Where would I get the entry fee? Stop paying the power bill? Take out a second mortgage? Set up a lemonade stand at the end of the driveway? I'm already totally underwater."

"Clancy said he'd cover the entry fee." Logan looked conflicted, and Tabby wasn't sure what her own face was doing.

"Out of the goodness of his heart?"

"He wants the buyer to see what I can do. He thinks it will ratchet up my price. It's in his best interest, and our best interest, too."

Clancy.

"Your cousin took me to the cleaners," Tabby reminded him. "You haven't spoken to him all summer. Tell me, why would we trust him?"

"Because we need money," Logan said frankly. "Because I think he wants to make things right, in his own twisted sort of way. Because I don't know how else to keep child services from taking Franzi away when I run out of money, which I'm about to. To keep what we have here…"

He came around the island to look earnestly down at her. Tabby desperately wanted to reach up and brush that lock of white back from his face, not that it would stay. She turned to the produce on the counter and began sorting it to keep her hands busy while Logan went on.

"It's *my fault* you're in this position. Not just the money I let Clancy swindle out of you. I looked up the Airbnbs in this area. You should be making hundreds of dollars a day and you're letting me completely freeload instead. I don't know how to repay you without doing this."

Tabby told herself to stop thinking of ways that he could repay her. They were strictly professional. She pulled a knife out of the butcher block and started thin-slicing cucumbers. "You said it wasn't illegal."

"Technically. It's a perfectly good aboveboard livestock sale when it occurs. But when I'm a human, it's no longer, you know, a *valid* sale because slavery isn't a thing anymore, so they can't own me and I'm free to go."

Tabby paused her knife. "You're arguing that because the law doesn't know about shifters and account for your sheer weirdness, it's an ethical thing to do?"

Logan shook his head. "It's not ethical," he agreed firmly. "I don't feel great about it. But I'm desperate. I could lose Franzi if child services started poking into my finances. I've already run through my savings. You could lose the ranch. I…could lose you."

It was hard to cling to morals when he was standing that close, looking that impassioned. Tabby sliced the cucumber coins in half and swept them into a bowl. "Do you solemnly swear that the guy you'd be scamming—conning—has enough money that it won't matter, *and* that he's a douchebag?"

"He won't even *notice* the money. And he deserves much, much worse. Whatever else Clancy is good at, he has a gift for finding scumbags."

"If we won the Grand Prix pot, why would we bother selling you?"

"Clancy will only front the entry fee if he gets to do the sale afterwards."

"Does he keep the money from the sale?"

"Twenty percent. It's a reasonable agent fee."

"And *I'd* keep the purse?"

"One hundred percent."

Tabby put a head of lettuce on the cutting board and started shredding it, trying to make sense of the offer. "It would mean I couldn't show you after that, if I've officially sold you. Everyone would recognize you after we did the Prix, and I couldn't risk someone seeing you here and word getting back to whoever bought you and lost you."

"We knew this couldn't last forever. You could buy the jumper that I was supposed to be if you want to keep showing once your ranch is established. You're a *great* rider, and a *great* trainer. You could find a horse as good as Beau."

"But it wouldn't be *you*," Tabby pointed out. She was destroying the lettuce head and endangering her fingers. Very quietly, she added, "You wouldn't be mine."

Logan reached out to take the knife from her. "Tabby…I will *always* be yours."

Tabby thought that it was the sound of her heart pounding in her throat, waiting for him to close that final distance and kiss her when there was a sudden crash from the dining room.

"I'm okay!" Franzi called.

20

How did parents of four-year-olds *ever* get laid? Logan wondered as he burst into the dining room to see what Franzi had destroyed.

Every time he thought that he would get Tabby alone, that he had a chance to make a move, that she *wanted* him to make a move, there was a disaster or a disruption.

Maybe this one was for the best, though, because Logan didn't want to influence her decision with seduction, even if he couldn't see a single alternative to their entangled financial dilemmas.

Franzi was lying on her back next to the chair she had clearly collided with, giggling at the ceiling. "I'm DIZZY!" she said.

Logan picked the cushion up off the chair and dropped it on her. She curled around it, kicking her legs and laughing, just as the timer went off.

"It'll have to cool down," Tabby called from the kitchen. "You've got a few minutes!"

The casserole wasn't the only thing that needed to cool down, Logan thought.

Tabby brought out the bowl of salad she'd mangled while he made the business proposal and gave Logan a hard look. "I have to think about the opportunity you offered me," she said very carefully.

"Of course." Opportunity was all that Logan really wanted with her. The opportunity to kiss her and lay her down on a quilt-covered bed. The opportunity to make her cry out his name and beg him to take her…

"I'm hungry," Franzi said, standing up to tug on Logan's hand.

"Let's pour drinks," Logan proposed. "You get the cups. One at a time! I'll get the ice and you can put the cubes in." He was going to need extra ice cubes in his pants.

~

*I*t took more than an hour to get Franzi into bed after dinner.

First she had to go potty, and then she needed a drink.

"There's a sippy cup by your bed," Logan reminded her.

"It's not cold enough," Franzi explained.

Logan put a few more ice cubes in it and tucked her back in, putting the favored stuffies all along her side. "They'll keep you warm and safe," he told her.

"Too hot," Franzi protested.

"I've got the window open," Logan pointed out. "Stick a leg out and it will cool down soon."

"Will you sing me a song?"

Logan sat at the edge of her bed, displacing a stuffed ray, and sang her the Pickles in a Jar lullaby. She corrected him every few stanzas as he tried to rush through it.

"Now you have to go to sleep," Logan said firmly as he bent down to kiss her forehead. "I love you, goodnight."

"I wuv you, too," Franzi said, tired.

For a moment Logan had hope, but when he got to the door, she called him back. "Uncle LOGAN! I need another hug!"

Logan was powerless against her request and bent to embrace her. "Go to sleep," he said. "No more hugs. No more water."

"Are you going to send me back?" Franzi asked in a tiny voice.

Logan kissed her forehead again. "Never," he promised. "Not ever. I'll be here in the morning and forever."

"Forever," Franzi agreed, her voice fading.

Logan leaned against her door after he closed it, waiting for her to call him back in. He had to keep her. He *pwomised*.

And he didn't know another way to keep that promise.

The stairs out of the stable apartment creaked as he walked down them, and Logan paused at the bottom looking up at her window to see if Franzi would wake up and cry out again.

When she didn't, he heaved a sigh and marched for the farmhouse. He couldn't do any of the noisy outdoor work, and it was too dark to paint, but he could snake the slow drain in the laundry room.

Tabby was standing on her front porch, her hands uncharacteristically still on the railing.

"I was going to take care of the laundry drain," Logan said, coming to the bottom of the steps but not offering to come up.

"I'll do it," Tabby said.

"The drain?"

"The show. The con."

"Are you sure?"

"I don't know what else to do." Tabby's voice in the darkness cracked, and Logan was up the steps before he could stop himself, gathering her into his arms where she belonged.

"We'll find another way," he said. "We can work something out. I'll…get another job, or live in a stall so you can rent our rooms out, or…"

"I'll do it," Tabby said, more determined. "It's a solid plan. It solves a lot of problems at once. I'm dying to do the show with you anyway. I'll do it."

He didn't remember consciously leaning down to her mouth, but somehow she was there under his lips, and he had one hand on the small of her back, the other cradling her jaw. Her mouth was soft and hot, eagerly meeting his and opening in welcome and need.

Kissing Tabby was everything that Logan knew it would be. She tasted like coffee and—

Hay! his stallion exclaimed. *Delicious sun-warmed hay!*

She does not taste like hay, Logan protested. But she *did* taste delicious, and Logan could not kiss her enough now that he had started.

"I need you to remember that you're mine when I sell you," she said, when she drew away for breath. "You're *mine.*"

"And you're *mine,*" Logan said in return, almost growling it. "Mine *forever.*" The words surprised even him, but they tasted right in his mouth.

After so long, sure he couldn't have her the way he wanted, Logan was ready to burst with his banked need. He kissed her harder, and twined his fingers into her hair. Her whole body was along his, hot and soft and strong, and her hands were up underneath his shirt, clawing at his back with her short, neat nails.

He pressed her back against the porch rail and it gave an ominous creak. "Not here," she gasped. "My bedroom."

Logan bent down and swept her up off her feet, surprising a laugh from her. "What are you doing?" she demanded, wrapping her arms around his neck. "You can't carry me!"

"I'm a shifter," Logan said, determined not to drop her. "I'm about to show you what that means."

"Well, you'd better do it with a condom," Tabby said, in her imminently practical way. "I've got some in my bedside table and hopefully they aren't expired."

Logan got her into the bedroom and down on the bed, where he kissed her longer and they touched each other eagerly. He got his hands up under her shirt, and peeled it off without unbuttoning. The top button popped off entirely.

He kissed all the exposed flesh above her bra, stroking her arms and her side as she squirmed beneath him. "Logan," she whispered, and every time she said his name, it seemed to settle into his skin a little deeper. He was Logan with her, not any of the dozens of other names he'd lived under. Just Logan.

"My Tabby," he said in return. "*Mine*."

He got her pants off first, taking the underwear with them in one move. She sat to remove her bra while he finished stripping, and he hesitated before he turned back to her. His cock was at attention, but there was a moment of uncertainty in new nudity, and Logan always wondered if it would come with disappointment because of the phrase *hung like a horse*. He was average, he knew from multiple adolescent measurements and an abundance of

Internet research, but his expectations were always tempered by what he'd seen in erotic media.

Tabby only looked pleased and excited, and when she reached out to touch him, Logan completely forgot to be self-conscious.

She stroked him and gently squeezed his balls and Logan bent to kiss her, crawling to cover her.

"Condom," she reminded him breathlessly, and there was a flurry of housekeeping that left him covered.

Then he was on her again, and she was spreading her legs as he drove into her, deeper and harder with every stroke. She came with flattering speed, crying out and arching underneath him so soon that Logan had a moment of doubt, wondering if she was exaggerating her pleasure. But there was no faking the flush in her chest or the heat and slick moisture between her legs. If she was acting, she was a much better actress than Logan had ever suspected even existed.

His reservations vanished as he continued to ride her, coaxing more noises of desire from her as he wrestled back his own impulse for release. The moment she seemed to be enjoying it less, he rolled to pull her over him, changing their angle and unlocking new satisfaction. She came again, her whole body clenching as he held her hips, except for her breasts, which swung freely.

Logan lost what was left of his control at her cries of joy, and felt his own wave break as she slowed and he clutched at her desperately and came at last.

She collapsed onto his chest and Logan wrapped his arms around her and held on as long as she let him, drinking in the smell and feel of her as their last aftershocks of sex ebbed away. "Mine," he said, stroking her hair, but he let her go when she stirred for freedom.

They cleaned up and when Tabby reached for her

underwear, Logan caught it and pulled it away. "Let me touch you a little longer," he begged, and Tabby stepped into the circle of his arms and let him pull her down onto the mussed bed.

Even sated, he could not get enough of the feel of her in his arms. She was so strong, and so feminine, a cluster of contradictions in the sexiest package that Logan had ever imagined. She was so capable and so independent, and so fragile and sweet. Her silky hair smelled like horse and sex and flowers and cedar.

She smells like a mate, Logan's stallion said with complete happiness. *Our mare.*

Logan let his arms tighten around her in surprise. Mates were a shifter girl's whispered nonsense, like fairy tales and happy endings…and yet here, with Tabby in the circle of his arms, he could imagine nothing more real and true.

She completed him the way he couldn't imagine anyone else ever doing, and she seemed to smooth over all his rough places and weeping wounds. He'd started their relationship with betrayal, and she'd countered it with trust. He came staggering into her life with an unexpected four-year-old and no means, and she'd given him a safe home and put his heart back together. If it wasn't for her, he wasn't sure what kind of guardian he could be to Franzi. If it wasn't for her, he'd have given up on everything that made him happier than he ever thought he could be.

He didn't deserve her—he couldn't!

But somehow, she was his.

"*Mine,*" he whispered into her hair, and he could feel her whole body smile in joy as she snuggled against him.

21

"You probably can't stay," Tabby said, when she had to decide between getting up and trying to fold the quilt over them from the far side of the bed to cover her goosebumped arms.

She didn't want to disturb the perfect equilibrium she felt, wrapped in Logan's arms, but she knew that shivering and letting her teeth chatter would be horribly unromantic.

"I left Franzi's window open," Logan said. "But I'm not sure it would wake me up from here."

"You're a good dad," Tabby said. "Or uncle. Whatever."

Logan squeezed her even tighter, but let her go when Tabby's chill was too much to ignore and she had to squirm free. "This doesn't change our agreement," she said. She regretted the words at once. Did she have to be a *complete* killjoy?

"Did I undersell my talents?" Logan asked rakishly, rolling onto his back and putting his hands behind his head. "Because I'm pretty sure you appreciated that."

Tabby flushed as she yanked her pants up on one leg

and nearly fell over. She remembered making plenty of noise and hoped that Franzi was a heavy sleeper. "I did appreciate that," she said.

Logan sat up and managed to look solemn and not at all cold, which was completely unfair. "I swear, I will repay you every penny that was taken from you, and continue to work for my keep as long as you'll have me, *however* you want me."

Tabby got the other leg of her pants on without humiliating herself and bent to kiss Logan on the forehead. "I'll keep you around," she said warmly. Logan tipped his head up at the last minute and what she'd meant to be a chaste kiss to keep things from being too cool between them turned into a lingering kiss on his talented mouth.

"I refuse to be tempted into forgiving your debt," she said, kissing him again and sitting in his lap.

"I can be very persuasive," Logan teased. "Would you like another demonstration?"

Tabby wrenched herself away before she could be tempted back. "The night is young," she said. "And the drain in the laundry room still needs snaked."

"You sure you don't need something else snaked?" Logan caught her hand, but only held it and didn't pull her back down, to her mixed disappointment.

"Don't get cocky with me, cowboy," Tabby warned him as she took back her hand and finished getting dressed. "And don't read…too much into this." She was mindful of Logan's advice about lying. *Know what they want and give them just enough of that.* Logan, she was sure, wanted a physical relationship with no strings. And wasn't that what she wanted, too? It felt good, but was it anything more? She didn't want to upset the delicate balance they had. Their working relationship was solid, and she didn't want to lose it by being clingy.

"Of course not," Logan said, even if he was watching her with appreciation. It was mutual—when he got up to get dressed, Tabby caught herself watching him with hunger that she thought she'd sated.

Tabby told herself that the possessive way he'd said *Mine* was just a thing that guys said, and she wished she had magical instinct to tell her what to do next. "Tell me more about instinct," she said, because she was definitely not going to admit that she was dreaming about true love and happy ever afters. "Is it like a spidey sense?"

"It can be," Logan said, getting his clothing on far more gracefully than Tabby had managed. "Sometimes, it's a sort of a vague good or bad feeling that's hard to pinpoint. Like, is it a bad idea to go that way because the road is flooded, or because you won't meet someone you otherwise might, or you'll save three second going the other direction? It doesn't ever overwhelm my free will, though sometimes I'll end up in an argument with my horse over it."

"Your horse is a separate voice in your head?" Tabby wondered if she should be worried about shifter mental health and split personality. "I just thought it was a...thing you could do."

"No, he's definitely got his own opinions and personality. Some shifters have pretty quiet animals, but I lucked out with one who has a lot to say. It makes conversing out loud challenging some times when I've got him trying to discuss the merits of alfalfa inside my head at the same time."

Tabby chuckled. "I have enough trouble tracking conversations when I'm hungry all by myself. Do you shifters all have a secret handshake?"

"It's hard to explain to someone who isn't one," Logan said. He opened the bedroom door and stood courteously aside for her. "We do recognize each other, when we're close enough, but it's...it's like explaining a smell to someone with no nose."

"That's a lovely mental image, thanks," Tabby scoffed. "Very romantic." She winced. She shouldn't be bringing up *romance* now. This *wasn't* romance.

But when she walked past Logan out into the living room, he patted her on the ass, and she found that she didn't mind. She also didn't mind when he kissed her on the porch, and again in the laundry room.

The drain did eventually get snaked...and something else did, also.

2 2

---

*L*ogan felt like he was trick-riding a runaway stallion. Everything seemed to be falling perfectly into place, but he knew that if he stopped moving or sneezed at the wrong time, it might all fall apart. He gave the rest of his savings to Cherry at Tiny Paws for the month and Tabby got the drill company to give her a month's respite before they sent her collections.

Franzi continued to blossom at the day care, and talked enthusiastically about her best friends and imaginary games. (It wasn't actually possible that one of the babies could teleport, was it?)

The playdate on the Fourth of July was a swimming success and Logan was sure that nothing would top the memory of Franzi as a foal frolicking with a strange dragon-deer-unicorn that seemed to skim across the surface of the grass. The offer had been extended again for Labor Day, the next holiday. In return, Vivian had agreed to take Franzi for a few nights while Tabby and Logan entered the three-day Grand Prix. Logan hadn't been clear with her about the fact that he was competing *as* the horse, but he thought that Vivian suspected as much. She didn't seem to judge him for it.

Mason seemed happy with his work at the auto shop, and Logan felt more and more like he was part of the team. Mason would call Logan over to watch tricky jobs, and explain what he was doing as he went. It wasn't officially a mentorship yet, but Logan knew he was on the right track. Cautious acquaintanceships had warmed to what Logan tentatively believed were friendships.

And *Tabby*.

As a horse, she worked him harder than ever in the arena, squeezing every ounce of speed and height out of him. "Sure, you got over it, but your last steps were a little close together. You could do better. Go again! Don't toss your head at me, you're not Fabio and it screws up your gait!" She took him out on hour-long rides to return sweating and springy. Logan knew that he was in the best shape of his life…and only some of his workout was in Tabby's bed.

At every chance they got, Logan was catching Tabby to kiss her, plucking at her clothing and making sure that she knew how badly he wanted her. And to his delight, she was eager for his touches as he was, even if she was irreproachably clear that it was purely a physical relationship.

Logan knew he was lucky to have that much from her, and he kept his stallion's desire to declare their undying love at every opportunity squelched. It was just scratching an itch.

Speaking of itches, hay was not the best place to make love.

"I have it *everywhere*," Tabby said with regret, pulling strands from unspeakable places a few days before the big show. The auto shop was closed for a local holiday, but the day care was open, so Logan intended to catch up on outstanding chores while he could do it without a forty-pound shadow complicating every task. "What was I thinking?"

"You were thinking that you can't resist me," Logan said merrily. "That you were willing to weather any discomfort for the pleasure I bring you. That I could take you to hedonistic heights you'd only imagined and that it would be worth it to get a little hay in your underwear."

Tabby buttoned her shirt with a blushing laugh. "Well, you aren't *wrong*," she conceded. "Even if you are pretty full of yourself."

"Are you ready for this?" Logan asked.

"If you want to go again, it will be in a *bed*," Tabby said tartly, buttoning her shirt. "I have regrets."

Logan caught her hand and pulled her back down in the straw with him. "I meant the show. The sale. Is this…okay?"

Logan had convinced himself that it was the best—the only—chance that he had to make a clean start and keep the life that they'd started to carve out for themselves. He was absolutely clear with Clancy that this was their last job and Clancy seemed to accept Logan's new resolve.

But Logan still had reservations, and if Tabby was the tiniest bit uncertain…

"I'm ready," Tabby said, rolling to kiss him. "I'm so ready. I don't know how we can't win. You're a gorgeous horse and smarter than your average bear. You can jump over *anything*. They won't know what hit them. Selling you completely solves your double life as my stallion, and even if he double-crosses you and your sale lines Clancy's pockets and not ours, the prize money should get us through until we can build the rest of the business. We'll keep our ranch."

"I'll miss you riding me," Logan said, stroking her hip.

Tabby kissed him deeply. "Oh, I don't think you *will*," she promised, her voice husky.

"Miss Swiftwater?"

Letisha's voice from outside the stable had Tabby rolling off of him and settling the last of her clothing in place as Logan rose and snatched his pants from the stall divider.

"I'll be right out!" Tabby called. To Logan she explained, "I'm going with Letisha and her mom to look at a horse they want to buy with their vet. A sound horse isn't necessarily a show horse, and they want a second opinion."

Logan followed her out of the stable, cursing the bits of grass that hadn't all been removed from his jeans and his shirt. Tumbles in the hay were definitely off the list.

Better for eating, his stallion sniffed.

Tabby left the stable with Letisha, already talking about the things she looked for in a horse. "It's unlikely you'll find one that's the whole package, like Beau," she cautioned, "but you want one with good sense and a willingness to listen and learn. It's more important that they move easily and have a brain than that they have perfect markings or measurements. You can't ride color!"

Logan's brain caught up with him as he watched Tabby walk away with Letisha hanging on her every word. She had said *our ranch.*

*We'll keep **our** ranch…*

It was *her* ranch, of course, but Logan found himself with spring in his step as he went to tackle the chores. He wanted all of the *us* and *ours* with Tabby.

She is part of our herd, his stallion said. *Of course she is ours and we are us.*

Logan was still trying to parse the pronouns when his phone rang.

"Logan," he said cheerfully, without looking at the screen first.

Clancy's voice always made him tense but even Clancy couldn't dampen Logan's joy. "I want to make sure we're still on for this weekend and you aren't going to pussy out on me," Clancy said tersely. "You haven't let her talk you out of it, have you?"

"We're in," Logan said. *We're. We!*

espite all of Tabby's outward confidence, she was painfully nervous, and she knew that Logan would feel it through her knees.

This wasn't just a country show or a state fair demonstration. She was competing against the best horses and riders in the state.

But they weren't riding *Logan.*

He nickered and nudged her reassuringly as she checked all of his straps again. The last thing she needed to do was fall off like an amateur in front of everyone because her tack had failed. She'd seal her ranch's fate and humiliate them both, kibosh the sale, and end up in the poorhouse after all.

The smaller shows they'd done had been casual and inclusive, but this was a bigger show, with a bigger prize. The other riders all seemed to already know each other. They swirled around in little cliques chatting about their TikTok channels and trips to Europe. Tabby smiled at them and got chilly nods in return. She had pinned her hair neatly back under her helmet, but hadn't remembered to put on makeup and she knew that no amount of polish could perfectly hide the scuffs on her worn boots.

The worst part of it was seeing Veronica Chase walk by, garbed in a designer jacket and boots.

Her fleeting hope that Veronica wouldn't recognize her was squashed when the woman paused at Logan's stall as Tabby did some last-minute touches to his mane. "Oh, *Swiftwater* Ranch," she said condescendingly to a rider giggling beside her. "I wouldn't do business with *them*. Very…second-rate, you know?"

"Pretty horse, though," her companion said diffidently. They both seemed determined to ignore Tabby, though she was standing right there brushing the same part of Logan's mane over and over.

"Pretty isn't everything," Veronica sniffed. "Breeding matters. They let anyone into these competitions, I swear. Anyway, they are only doing the jumper courses, not the hunter trials, so beauty doesn't do them any good." The two strolled past, snickering.

Tabby caught herself grimacing when Logan tipped his head into her shoulder reproachfully. He'd undoubtedly heard the woman's snipe.

"We've still got this," she reminded herself. They couldn't say a word against her gorgeous horse, but Tabby herself was an easy target. It was a common tactic among the truly competitive to work to make other riders nervous. A nervous rider made mistakes and gave their horse mixed messages.

A nervous rider *lost*.

When the hunter princesses had passed out of earshot, continuing to lament the fact that the board let just anyone compete, Logan snorted and swiftly shifted.

"What are you doing?" Tabby asked, though she didn't

protest when Logan pressed a kiss on her mouth. "You can't be caught like this!"

"I wanted to tell you before you were called up, I'm not the only shifter."

"*What?*"

"I sensed them when you led me in. We're not the only ones trying to pull a fast one here. This isn't a level playing field at all."

Tabby steamed. "Did Clancy know that?"

"Probably. I don't know what his long game is. We can still win it, though. We're a good team."

They were, Tabby agreed, and she gave him a lingering kiss until a rattle at the far end of the stable had Logan stepping back from her and shimmering into horse form. She checked his tack for a fourth time.

Any lingering reservations that she'd had regarding the ethics of riding Logan in a competition vanished in the wake of her chilly reception and the knowledge of the stacked deck. The other shows had been sporting competitions full of warmth and welcome, but everyone here had come to win at any cost. It was clear that she was considered a threat to be frozen out and taken down.

Nothing made Tabby dig in her heels more than unkindness.

Clancy was waiting outside the arena by the mounting block. Tabby steeled herself for an unpleasant encounter, but he was clearly on his company behavior, all slick smiles and flattering attention. Although he had some similar features, he was less handsome than his cousin, Tabby thought, like a cheap knock-off.

"What a beautiful pair you two make," Clancy said, with the same silky voice that had sold her Logan in the first place. "I'm sure you'll wow them all."

Tabby let Logan shuffle forward and stomp threateningly in the sand by Clancy's foot.

Clancy didn't flinch, but he did frown a little. "Temper, temper," he said. "You *know* this is a solid plan." To Tabby, he said slyly, "You should have kept his original name."

Tabby kept herself from snapping that Clancy was the one who'd *better behave*.

Logan heaved a sigh and sidled into place by the mounting block. Tabby climbed up and settled into the saddle. Would this be her last chance to ride Logan?

24

*W*hatever else went wrong in the world, it always felt right to have Tabby on his back.

Logan felt better with the press of her long legs and the feel of her hand on his neck, patting him like he was an animal that needed reassurance.

His stallion snorted. *You **are** an animal that needs reassurance. You like to think you're better than me, but you're just as basic, and you need your herd.*

Logan ignored him, and let Tabby ride him in to the waiting pen as the rider before them finished the course on their final day.

He used his watch-without-watching trick to observe them carefully. It was one of the shifter horses that he'd sensed on his way in, and while the pair did a better-than-average job because of the mare's human senses, she was not the jumper that Logan was.

More telling, her rider was mediocre at best, and the horse couldn't compensate for all of their failings. Several times, she had to give a little hitch to keep her rider balanced, and there were times that the rider was giving messages that the mare was ignoring. She was showy, but faulted several times and her rider was clearly the weak point. Logan bounced in place and felt Tabby settle in her seat. He wouldn't have that problem.

The pair went off, disqualified, and Logan was more confident than ever. He shook his head and felt Tabby give-take the reins in rebuke.

When their name was called, she guided him forward and let him step out freely, using all of his long stride to best advantage.

They had done a test walk through on the course before the competition, so Logan already knew what to expect and how to place his feet. He cleared every rung that was put up, and soared over the water long-jumps with inches to spare.

His stallion was singing in his head, pleased to have all of the attention on them, glad to have a rider that could show them off so perfectly. *We are grace and beauty!* he cried. *Everyone should admire us!*

Tabby's tireless drilling kept them moving between the jumps like water. No motion was wasted, and being airborne with her was like making music.

They ended to more enthusiastic applause than any previous rider had received and Logan felt a rush of pride and delight that wasn't just his stallion's.

They'd done it.

It didn't even require a jump off, his win had been so clear and clean. Veronica Chase, disqualified early, watched them accept their prize with a sour look.

Tabby dismounted and took Logan on a cool-down walk before returning to his stall to be groomed and watered.

Clancy was already there with a collection of well-dressed investors and was passing himself off as Tabby's agent. "Ah, here is Miss Swiftwater, hero of the hour, and the beautiful Beau."

Logan did a masterful act of arching his neck and keeping his steps fresh and springy, like the course had taken nothing out of him and he was ready to go out and do it again.

"You're thinking of selling him?" one of the men asked speculatively.

"I'd *consider* selling him to the right buyer," Tabby answered coyly, just as they had practiced. "He's a valuable asset to my ranch. Oh, here's my card. I do have training, boarding, and lesson openings."

25

"**A**m I an awful person?" Tabby asked as she rubbed Logan down and took off his tack after Clancy left with the men to talk contracts and details. "Should I feel worse about winning?" She felt giddy and weirdly let down. She'd won, but did she *deserve* it? It soothed her conscience that other horses in the ring had been shifters, but she wasn't sure it completely excused it. Schadenfreude was complicated.

Three quarters of a ton of horseflesh suddenly shifted into a man right in front of her and Tabby gave a squeak of alarm as she glanced out at the aisle of the stable. The stall door was shut, but there were other riders talking loudly at the far end of the building and going about the care of their horses.

"What are you doing, Logan?" she hissed. "Someone could come by at any moment!"

Logan, with apparently no care for being caught, scooped her up into an embrace. "I had to tell you that you were amazing and that we *earned* that win. I didn't do anything supernatural and you were *perfect*. You aren't allowed to feel bad about rubbing Veronica Chase's perfectly made-up face in manure of her own making."

"I had a better horse," Tabby admitted, kissing him back. "Much, much better."

"I had a better rider," Logan insisted. "Much, much better."

How did Logan always make everything feel alright?

"I wish you were coming back with me," Tabby said. "I know just how to celebrate our win."

"Maybe Clancy will fumble the deal," Logan said, kissing down the side of her neck. "Then I could come straight back with you."

"Is that likely?" Tabby said hopefully.

"Not really," Logan said. "He wouldn't have sprung for the entry if he wasn't sure about the outcome."

Tabby was nearly ready to risk a tumble in itchy hay, his touches were so skilled and Tabby was already all worked up from adrenaline and excitement. Surely, it wouldn't be too bad if they put down a coat…

She knocked his hat back off of his head so she could at least kiss him more properly.

"No!" Tabby drew back at the sound of Veronica Chase's angry voice as she suddenly stalked past the stall speaking loudly into her phone. "I am *not* waiting for him to come around. I want that property on the market before the end of the month so we can flip it before the fiscal quarter ends—" The realtor glanced to the side just in time to meet Tabby's eyes and see her standing kissing distance to Logan. Logan stooped to pick up his hat and tipped it to her in what felt like slow motion as Veronica continued past after the barest startled and angry pause.

"—I'm not interested in your excuses," she continued as she stomped away. "I've had enough *excuses* today."

"Whew," Tabby said, leaning into Logan's arms as Veronica's shrill voice faded down the aisle. She hadn't seen anything too incriminating. Yes, Logan was standing in a stall where a horse ought to be, but there were a lot of reasons that her horse might be somewhere else. The most suspicious thing was the white lock in Logan's dark hair that had first clued Tabby in to his dual nature. She brushed it up under his hat. "Have you ever thought about dyeing that?"

Logan chuckled. "My horse would never let me."

"Is it possible that he has more vanity than *you* do?" Tabby teased. She sighed. "You should shift back while it's clear. Clancy will be back soon." She stepped back into his embrace before he could. "I'm…going to miss you."

Logan kissed the top of her head and rubbed her shoulders. "I'll be back before you know it," he murmured.

It was an *I love you* moment, Tabby recognized, breathing in the smell of him and the comfort of his cotton shirt over his muscular chest. But were they there yet? Did he even feel the same way? Sometimes he still joked about paying off his debt with great sex, but was it *all* in jest? He was as complicated as schadenfreude.

"I have a sale to close, and it's not with that ugly mug."

Clancy's voice outside the stall set Tabby back on edge. She gave Logan one lingering last kiss, not caring that Clancy was watching over the door.

"Last gambit," Logan said warningly to his cousin when he was done kissing Tabby. "Nothing else after this."

"That's what you said," Clancy smirked. Did he not believe that it was Logan's last con? Should Tabby be doubtful, too? "Anyway, I've all but closed the deal. My buyer's agent wants to take you now, and he's on his way, so shape up, Logan, and get your signing pen ready, Miss Swiftwater." His voice filled with warning.

"I'm ready," Tabby said.

She told herself that she didn't have instinct, so there was no real reason for the dread in her heart.

---

26

*L*ogan ignored the sizzle of instinct that told him he was doing the wrong thing. He was used to thinking that Clancy's plans were a bad idea. Was this really any different? He was just sad to say goodbye to Tabby for any length of time. That was the only reason that the pressure seemed worse than ever behind his eyes. He'd just be gone two days, three at the most.

Wrong, his stallion murmured. *Wrong, wrong, wrong.*

It's just temporary, Logan assured him. *We've been sold before. It always works out.*

Neither his horse nor his instinct settled in the slightest as Tabby signed him away and kissed his nose goodbye.

Something is WRONG, his horse insisted, and for a moment, it was an actual struggle to keep them walking forward when Clancy led him up the ramp into the horse trailer.

It's just a horse trailer, Logan insisted. *No worse than any other horse trailer.* It was actually a lot nicer than a lot of horse trailers he'd been in, with room for multiple animals, even if Logan seemed to be the only passenger.

Wrong, his stallion growled back, stamping their foot.

Let it go, Logan said soothingly, letting Clancy hook him up to the trailer tie. *We'll take a nice little ride to a swanky stable, have a bunch of oats and fresh hay and as soon as it's safe, we'll shift and get an Uber home.*

"Have a good ride, cousin," Clancy said. "Thanks for making this so easy." He slapped Logan on the flank and left, pausing to have a brief conversation with a man outside the trailer.

Logan wasn't sure why Clancy's words felt so ominous. Maybe Clancy had gotten a bigger cut than he'd let on. Logan shrugged. Clancy could have the money from his sale. Tabby had the prize money and a number of potential new clients. *It's a good plan*, he told his horse.

WRONG, his stallion insisted.

The horse trailer wasn't just bigger, but also better sprung than the conveyances he used with Clancy, so it was a smoother ride than Logan expected. He forced his misgivings aside and spent the trip drowsing and thinking about Tabby, about living on her ranch and raising Franzi together. They hadn't talked about what happened next with them, but Logan liked the idea of settling down. Would she want to get married?

Logan had to laugh at the change his life had taken. Logan of just a few months ago would never have imagined this kind of domestic happiness. Now he had a little girl and a lot of big dreams.

It was a long trip and Logan was grateful when the highway finally gave way to a winding driveway that opened to a palatial estate that he could just glimpse through the horse trailer window. Unnaturally green lawns carpeted landscaped slopes, and a sprawling mansion overlooked a whole cluster of buildings. Logan counted at least seven garage doors as they went through a gate, and saw the sparkle of a swimming pool through a courtyard.

This is how the other half lives, he thought.

At one point, it was all he aspired to.

Now, he couldn't wait to get back to the comparatively brown scrub of Tabby's ranch. He'd rather have her pretty and plain land than a hundred of these fancy properties. The trailer pulled up beside a stable with a covered arena.

Logan shuffled a little in place out of habit.

"We got him!"

The agent who had closed the sale was the one who opened the back of the trailer and Logan rolled an eye to see who was standing beside him.

Shit.

Some jobs went so sideways that they were remembered forever, and this had been one of them.

Clancy had sold Logan to a horse enthusiast with deep pockets and good security, and it was because of the heat that the thwarted collector had put on them that Clancy had moved to smaller, weaker targets like Tabby.

Shit.

Adam Tallier was a big man with big, cruel hands and he was looking at Logan with a dangerously self-satisfied smirk.

"I've bought you twice now, *Logan,*" he said casually. "I'm not losing you again."

Logan's alarm escalated. How did this man know his real name? He resisted his impulse to tug at the lead or shift, keeping his neck soft and his feet still. He couldn't quite keep his tail from swishing in agitation.

It didn't matter what Tallier tried to do to him. In a day or two, he'd have an opportunity to escape and all of this would be behind him.

But Tallier had known *his name.*

What had Clancy told him? Why would he risk a sale to the *same person?*

WRONG! his stallion was screaming without stopping. *WRONG. WRONG. WRONG.*

At this point, Logan couldn't tell what was his horse's sheer panic and what was instinct, burning him like a poison oak rash. *What do you want me to do?* he asked impatiently.

Fight! Flee! Kick! his stallion offered.

Later, Logan wondered if that wouldn't have been the better option, but he stubbornly shoved both horse and instinct back. He would keep up the act, be docile and obedient. *Nothing but a horse in here,* he thought as hard as he could. *I'm just a big beast who wants to work.*

Who are you calling a beast? his stallion wanted to know, distracted from his panic by the insult.

Not you, Logan assured him. *We're just pretending.*

"Bring him," Tallier said, snapping his fingers.

The agent jumped to obey, unclipping Logan's lead and backing him down the ramp.

Logan saw no point in trying to escape, despite his stallion's whining, and wheeled in place to face Tallier with no hint of recognition or more than animal intellect.

"Show Logan his new accommodations," Tallier said with a smile.

The stable was sparkling clean and freshly painted. Logan found himself comparing it to Tabby's. It utterly lacked personality; everything was sterile white and modern chrome, with no dents or scratches. Not a strand of hay was out of place. His stall door had a keypad lock instead of a latch, which seemed ridiculous and clearly only for show. Tallier was the sort of billionaire who want the latest and greatest, even when it was pointless, and would only delay getting horses out in an actual emergency, but it allowed the stall design to include enough room for a face to squeeze through, since there was no mechanical latch a clever horse could puzzle out. No doubt it had been selected because it *looked* fancier.

But the keypad added no challenge to Logan, because he had his keypad cracker in his pocket. As a human, he could release himself as easily as if there *had* been a simple latch.

Logan cast an eye at the walls; he would be able to scale it easily as a man. The security was all designed to keep a horse inside.

To Logan's surprise, two men waited inside the stall and a smell made him step more slowly. Something was burning.

No, not burning, it was the smell of hot metal, like an overstressed engine. The agent had the lead on Logan and pulled him into a corner of the stall, so that Logan couldn't turn to figure out what it was without visibly resisting.

"Where do you want it, boss?"

"Left hip," Tallier said. "I want it visible."

Logan realized what must be happening and fought to get control of his head back in time to glance back and see one of the men stepping forward with what looked like a glowing metal brooch at the end of an iron stake.

WRONG! his stallion screamed as the metal touched his flank.

They were aligned in their protest and Logan kicked and bit and reared, but not before the brand seared into his flesh with a white-hot flash of pain.

It hurt so badly that Logan was disoriented, like he'd

just been kicked in the head himself, and his stallion took over, lunging and fighting.

The men scattered before him and the branding iron went flying to rattle off the wall and fall to the ground.

"Get out of here!" one of the men cried.

"Shit!"

Logan reared and struck the agent with his front hooves as he ripped his lead out of his hands. He rolled away before Logan could come down on him, and one of the other men dragged him out of the way as Logan staggered and turned. He got another kick in, and a mouthful of torn fabric before they tumbled out of his stall in a flat-out panic.

Tallier, safely back near the door of the stable, asked, "Did you get it on him?"

"He's marked," one of the men said, examining the part of his shirt that had been torn. Logan hoped he got a little flesh with it; he could taste something metallic in his mouth.

"Good work," Tallier said.

Logan charged the door and was pleased that everyone stepped back, even though he didn't do more than rattle it in place. He snorted and stomped, daring them to try him.

Tallier stepped forward a little, flushing like he was embarrassed that he'd been caught flinching. "Might as well settle in, Logan. You're here for good this time."

Logan spun and landed a double-barreled kick at the door, which only rattled in place.

The men seemed to relax, realizing that there was nothing he could do from inside his stall while Logan paced and tossed his head.

"He'll mellow out and get to work when he realizes he has no choice," Tallier said firmly. "Won't you, Logan."

I'd rather eat nails and spit them at you, Logan thought fiercely.

Then they were gone and Logan was alone in his stall. The stable was quiet except for the snuffling and shuffling of other equine inhabitants.

His flank *hurt*.

That sonofabitch branded me, Logan realized. He still felt fuzzy, like he'd been drugged, not just burned, and he was happy that his stallion had plenty of self-defense skills.

Wrong, his stallion said mournfully. *You're wrong.*

I know I was wrong to do this job, Logan snarled. *You don't have to rub it in.*

No, his stallion said. *You're **wrong** now.*

Logan was inclined to agree, even if he couldn't put his finger on what was off. Normally, he'd wait until night to make his escape, but finding that Tallier was his ultimate buyer worried him deeply. He would risk being stopped as a man to get out of here and back to Tabby and Franzi faster.

He thought about slipping his shape back to human and waited for his perspective to change as his height shrank.

Nothing happened.

Logan tried to rub his head with a human hand and just convulsed, dipping his head and lifting one hoof.

He was still a horse.

Shifting had never taken much effort. Even as a child, Logan had been adept at moving from one form to another, taking his clothes with him early and excelling at trick shifts that involved tossing something off his back to catch it in human hands.

He didn't know what to do when it simply didn't work.

He tried concentrating harder, around the pain

blooming on his hip and his forehead. If he could just focus…

He still had four feet.

What's wrong? he cried. *Why isn't it working?*

WRONG, was all that his stallion could reply.

ogan tested the strength of every wall and door with his feet, and found that the stall had been built to keep a strong and temperamental stallion in. Without human limbs and digits, and access to his keypad cracker, he was completely imprisoned.

He snuffled around the stall and found the iron that they'd seared him with, safely cooled in a pile of faintly charred hay. It was lucky that it hadn't started a fire. It still looked more like a brooch than a branding iron, welded at the end of an iron rod. It had too much fine detail to be a logo, and it looked a little like antlers that ended in knots when Logan nosed it around and fixed one of his eyes on it. It gave Logan a tingle of magical recognition, but he couldn't put a finger on what instinct was trying to tell him.

Because you don't have fingers, his stallion snorted.

It's an expression, you dolt, Logan sighed.

He tried again to pry the door open, or to get a grip with his teeth on the hinges, and failed. He could get his head over the stall door, but he couldn't reach the keypad, and he wasn't sure he could use his big tongue to push the buttons anyway. Assuming he could figure out the code or see it when he was that close.

Finally, he dozed as the night fell in earnest and morning followed it.

He wasn't the only horse in the stable, but none of the others had shifter tingles that he could sense. Grooms and stablehands came in and out to feed and clean them, occasionally taking one of the other horses out on a lead, but none of them approached Logan's stall. It probably didn't help that Logan had his head out over his door and was eyeing them dangerously and curling his lips in fury.

What he did notice, though, was that all the keypads had the same code.

It made sense; Tallier probably didn't have a staff that could remember a separate code for each valuable horse. As the afternoon turned into evening, Logan pieced together the access numbers, running them over in his head so he wouldn't forget them.

4-7-2-3-9

4-7-2-3-9

4-7-2-3-9… He kept wanting to continue the string with the numbers from the 80s song Jenny. If he could call someone, they could break him out…but his phone was in his human shifted pocket with the keypad cracker, and his calls were probably going to voicemail right now.

He still couldn't reach the keypad, and didn't have fingers to use on it, even if he could. He paced the stall, and kicked the unyielding door again.

"Temper, temper," Tallier said, catching him at his futile efforts that evening. He didn't offer to come within biting distance of the door, though. "I'm a patient man, Logan, and I can wait until you've realized your position here. A horse as *clever* as you could do a lot for a man like me, and you don't have any other choices now."

Logan howled in rage inside his head, but he only turned away in a show of disdain, his ears flat back and his tail twitching.

"Should we sedate him?" one of the stablehands asked.

"He won't hurt himself," Tallier said with a smirk. "He's too *smart* for that. He's got plenty of hay and water and he'll see the error of his ways soon enough."

They left, and Logan paced around the stall again, clipping the branding iron with one hoof.

The sound jogged an idea, and he reached down to take it into his mouth. With much effort, he could get it balanced, the tingling brooch inside his mouth and the iron rod sticking out like a cigar. The rod was about the width of a human finger.

It took an agonizing number of tries to figure out the angle, stretching his head out over the door as far as he could, that it would take to depress the keypad buttons with the rod, and he clumsily keyed in the code wrong four times before he accidentally dropped the branding iron from his numb lips.

Logan had to lay down in the straw and use one leg to paw the iron back under the door to himself, cursing inside his head until his stallion was as agitated as he was.

Hopefully the keypad didn't have a number of wrong inputs that would shut it down.

Twice as slowly and carefully, his neck at an agonizing angle, Logan punched in the code. 4-7-2-3-9.

Whirr!!

The door cracked open and Logan dropped the branding iron, crowding into the gap to make sure that it didn't accidentally close again.

Free! We're free! his stallion crowed.

Logan heard a commotion at the stable door and had to wrestle back his impulse to charge out regardless. He found the piece of cloth that he'd ripped from the unlucky handler and stuffed it with his mouth into the latch so it wouldn't fully close again, then pawed the rod back into his stall and closed the door, listening in dread for the sound of it clicking shut. If it didn't, would the colored light on the keypad give it away? Should he just let it close and hope he could open it again?

He finished as the grooms came in to do their last rounds. They didn't offer to come into Logan's stall, and didn't seem to notice if the keypad showed a different color. A new net of hay was slung in over the door.

Oh, that's good stuff, his stallion said, distracted by the tantalizing smell.

Logan snorted and stomped, threatening, and the staff moved on.

We should eat before we escape, his stallion said practically, moving to munch on it.

Logan remembered what the trainer had said about sedation. He didn't want to risk being muddled and sleeping through his chance to get out.

I'd know if it was wrong, his stallion insisted, and Logan let him eat.

It was hard to wait until night truly fell and all the sounds of the house went quiet. Logan knew that there would still be staff on duty, but he hoped that they would be looking out for things breaking in, and that surprise would be all the advantage he needed.

The door slid open silently when he tested it, and Logan felt himself sag in relief. He paused and took the detested branding rod up in his mouth. It had something to do with how he'd gotten stuck this way, and he wasn't going to leave it behind if he could help it.

It was worse than a bit, with hard edges and a rough iron surface that cut at Logan's already stressed lips, but he clamped it in his mouth and set out to escape the stall.

He feared that the stable would have a lock as well, but if it did, it was overruled by the fire exit style handle on the inside; a simple push with his knee and it swung open.

Unfortunately, it triggered an alarm that immediately began to blare.

Logan didn't pause, but stretched out into a full gallop as soon as he was clear of the doorway, gravel flying from his hooves.

What he hadn't considered was that the security staff on night duty would be armed, and that they might shoot at a valuable, prize-winning horse.

How dare they! his stallion shrieked in outrage.

It only put fresh urgency into Logan's flight, and he did a rodeo barrel horse justice with his zigzag pattern as he skidded off the driveway and into the darkness of the yard, bullets shredding leaves just off his flank.

Someone shouted and the shooting stopped, but flood-lights came on along the driveway. Logan took a chance and the straight shot, and flew back out of the darkness down the driveway at full speed, gathering himself as he saw the gate at the end.

Maybe he could have made it as a racehorse after all, he thought, hearing the noise fade away behind him. There was just a guardhouse at the end to get past, with an inef-fective crossbar that Logan sailed over with feet to spare. The gate guard watched him go with an open mouth.

Then Logan was pounding out onto the dark road and settling into a ground-eating gallop.

He heard vehicle doors and engines at the top of the drive behind him, and left the road to leap over a ditch and a fence and flee into the darkness across a field.

He kept running long after the sounds behind him faded to nothing, crashed through an orchard, and finally slowed in a second dark field. He had no direction sense besides *away*, and ran until his legs were aching and his sides were heaving.

They were free.

They were free and could return to Franzi and Tabby, who were expecting them home by now…and Logan had no idea which direction that was.

His phone, with GPS, was safely shifted with his unreachable human form, and Logan could be anywhere. He might not even be in Montana anymore. He couldn't exactly walk up to a gas station and ask for directions as a *horse*, and he wasn't sure how to unfold a map even if he could steal one.

His mouth was aching around the iron bar now, and after considering for a moment, Logan found a ditch to drop it into. He'd try to find his way back to it for answers, but at least Tallier wouldn't have it anymore.

He worked his sore lips and cut tongue as they trotted along the field road. Eventually, it would come out on a road or a driveway, and that would take him to a street or a highway. He could read street signs and hopefully find something familiar.

Instinct can help us, his stallion reminded him. *At least it can if you aren't going to be a stubborn ass about it.*

Logan was really good at ignoring instinct when it told him he was being dumb, and he often forgot to listen to it when it would help him. Humbled, he stopped, closed his eyes, and looked inside.

It wasn't a glowing path through the night to show him

where to go, and it wasn't quite a dowsing rod, but it *was* a gentle tug when he was finally still enough, and he let his feet follow it.

Franzi. Tabby. They were *that way.* They were calling him home.

2 8

Driving home without Logan was one of the hardest things that Tabby had ever done.

The prize money in her purse was small compensation for not having Logan to celebrate with on the drive back, and Tabby was not sure she had ever felt so *lonely*.

It's just for a couple of days, tops, she reminded herself.

They had a plan, and it was a good plan, and she already had a dozen contacts for boarding and training, and a dozen more business cards with private numbers scrawled on the back. She'd even found a sweet-natured mare she was interested in buying to train for shows, and a contractor who was willing to do some work in exchange for lessons for his horse-crazy daughter. The championship check would cover her outstanding bills with a little buffer, even before she saw her share of the horse sale.

It was a good job, Tabby told herself. *We **earned** the prize.* They'd even outstripped other shifters trying the same con. The memory of Veronica Chase's face alone was worth every effort.

But she couldn't shake the sense of loss that she felt

driving into her ranch without Logan, knowing that he wasn't there to be happy with her.

She'd feel better when he got out and came home, and the best thing she could do was stay busy until he did. It was only for a few days.

So Tabby fell to working. She tended the horses, who showed her how much they'd missed her by slobbering down her shirt and developing bizarre new fears of blowing leaves and crinkly plastic bags. Tabby soaked up their companionship and took them for long, indulgent rides, taking comfort in their familiar quirks and animal normalcy. There was nothing magical about mucking stalls and cleaning tack.

The next day, she followed up on every one of the new connections she'd made and wept in relief at the new boarding and training entries in her ledger. It might not be enough to declare complete solvency or pay off the entire mortgage, but after the prize money, she was back on solid ground.

She wished that Logan was there to squeal with and dance around the kitchen, but he didn't come back the next day.

Or the next.

Tabby told herself that it wasn't that Logan had taken his share of the sale and disappeared with them. He was probably…just held up. Maybe he'd taken Franzi to Disneyland. She only let herself call him twice, and was sent straight to voicemail. He wasn't even running any later than he said he would be yet, just later than he *hoped* he would be. Don't panic until day three, he'd said. Well, here was day three. Did she get to panic in the middle of it, or did she have to wait until the end?

She was in the garden, sweating through her shirt as she pulled weeds and tied up sprawling vines of peas and beans and cursed the rabbits, when her phone rang. "Swiftwater Ranch!" she said breathlessly, without looking at the number.

"Ah, hi. This is Vivian Wang, I'm sorry to bother you, but I'm looking for Logan Kennedy. I understand he lives there?"

Tabby caught her breath. "Yes," she squeaked.

"His daughter, er, niece, Franzi is staying over with my daughter Tara. Franzi says…well…we were expecting him to pick her up today, and he's not *that* late, but Franzi is very sure that something's…um…wrong and he's not answering his phone and I wondered if he was on his way yet?"

Tabby could hear the layers of code in Vivian's words. Instinct. Franzi's instinct was suggesting that Logan was in trouble. Tabby didn't have magical instinct to explain away her unease, but it was there anyway, and twice as strong with Vivian's careful words. She wasn't sure what she and Logan had, but if Logan was going to skip out, he wouldn't do it without Franzi. He adored that girl to the moon and back.

Something was *wrong*.

"I've been expecting him back, too," she said, the pit of her stomach feeling cold and heavy. "I'm not sure where he is. I can come get Franzi, though. He said he might be a day late. We probably shouldn't worry too much yet." She wasn't reassuring herself any.

Vivian hesitated, then said, "Tara says you're safe and Franzi should go home," she finally said. "Let me give you our address and I'll have Franzi pack up her suitcase."

Tabby forgot the car seat and had to turn around in her driveway to go back and get it out of Logan's truck. She forced herself to slow down several times on the way to Nickel City. She hated leaving the ranch if there was any chance that Logan would come back there. But she couldn't leave Franzi to impose on Tara's family any longer.

She worried that Vivian might have reservations about handing Franzi over to a stranger, but needn't have.

A tall, blue-eyed man answered the door, dressed in scrubs covered in dinosaurs and gave her a narrow-eyed assessment without speaking. Tabby worried how she measured up. She smelled like horse and hay and fresh paint, probably, and her hair was coming loose from her braid because she hadn't thought to fix it for company.

"Miss Tabby!" Franzi cried from inside the house, just as Tabby apparently passed muster and the man stepped aside to invite her in. "I'm Becket," he said kindly. "Franzi is about ready to go."

Vivian proved to be a soft but capable-looking woman juggling a baby, and Tara was a petite girl with Chinese features who looked like she was Franzi's age. She gave Tabby a look that was twice as judgmental as Becket's, then nodded her approval. "You have to go home," she said to Franzi.

"Uncle Logan will be home soon!" Franzi said firmly, dragging her suitcase behind her. Tabby stepped to take it from her. It was mostly full of blankets and stuffies and weighed almost nothing; Franzi just wasn't tall enough to carry it.

"Well, we'd better be there when he gets there," Tabby said. "Thanks for taking Franzi for a few days."

"How was the horse show?" Vivian asked, bouncing the baby, who didn't want to be held and was arching and stretching for freedom.

"It went really well," Tabby said honestly. She couldn't help adding, "We took home the prize." She and *Logan*.

"That's great!" Vivian cheered.

"We have to go now," Franzi insisted. "Tara says Uncle Logan will be home soon."

Tabby let herself be herded out of the door as she thanked them again for their hospitality and bemusedly loaded Franzi into the truck and slung the suitcase behind the seat.

"How do you know your uncle Logan will be home soon?"

"Tara knows," Franzi said confidently.

Did Tara have some larger kind of instinct to draw on?

Tara's certainly was apparently good enough for Franzi, and Tabby took some comfort in it.

To her disappointment, Logan wasn't there when they arrived back at the ranch. Tabby had Franzi bring her suitcase into the house in case she had to sleep there, and made them a quick meal of instant rice with hamburger and fresh vegetables cut up in it. She went to the window every time she heard a noise, but there was never anyone there.

"I've got a spare room you can sleep in," Tabby said, when it was clear that Franzi was running out of steam. It was fully dark now, and when she let herself try calling Logan again, it went straight to voicemail…and told her the box was full.

She made up the room for Franzi, who wanted to touch the model horses on the shelves.

"They aren't toys," Tabby cautioned. "They're…here, you can play with this one." It was her first model, missing an ear and part of its mane, and had been through some rough play in its life.

Franzi, who clearly knew she was being bought off with a substandard item, gave it a test gallop across the guest bed that Tabby uncovered. Then she carefully unpacked her suitcase and laid out her stuffies and blankets.

She took so long in the bathroom going potty that Tabby began to wonder if there was a problem, then took twice as long to brush her teeth. Finally, she was dressed in pajamas and Tabby could tuck her into bed.

"Uncle Logan will be back," Franzi said trustingly, as if Tabby was the one who was worried.

She was, she realized, and she hadn't realized what an excellent distraction Franzi was until the last of her little noises went silent.

Tabby risked a peek into the bedroom and Franzi was lying as if she'd fallen asleep in the act of rearranging her stuffies, one arm stretched out from under the blankets. Tabby tiptoed in and pulled the blanket up over her. She gave a happy little sigh.

Tabby left and closed the door. She went through her evening barn chores in an unhappy daze of worry.

Where was Logan? Why wasn't he back yet?

---

29

*E*ven with instinct to guide him and to warn him when someone's interest in a loose horse was more than just trivial, it was a complicated journey.

Logan had to cross a crowded highway once, waiting at the edge of the road for a gap in the traffic, and instinct gave a little twinge when a truck with a trailer slowed down and a man got out with a rope.

He risked a gap in the cars that he otherwise wouldn't have, and sailed over the concrete divider. Another truck had to slam on its brakes, and someone honked.

Logan didn't stop running until he'd found a copse of trees to get behind, cursing the brief open farm area with its unobstructed view.

Wild forest was too thick to travel through quickly, and fields were too exposed, so Logan found himself skirting the woods when he could. The landscape was full of unexpected ravines and craggy bluffs, as well as invisible animal holes that could easily break a horse's leg if they were running at full speed and went down.

Sometimes the magical sense was just gone, like a

smoke trail that had grown too faint to see or smell. Logan could do nothing but trot on in the direction he'd last been pointed and hope that he was still headed for Tabby's ranch when he had to detour around natural pitfalls and try to find his compass bearings again.

When it wasn't outright hazardous, the trip was tiring. Logan had a ground-eating trot on a smooth trail, but the terrain he covered was anything but easy. After a few hours, barely pausing to snatch enough grazing to go on, his muscles burned. He was grateful for Tabby's training and recognized how much worse it would have been if he'd been in the mediocre shape he'd considered good before he came to stay with her.

She was humbling, Logan thought, as he started diagonally across a field in the dark, ripe wheat whispering away from his flanks. He thought he'd been whole and had everything, and then he got Franzi and realized exactly how incapable he actually was. If it hadn't been for Tabby, he would have failed at everything.

Hel-lo, his stallion grumbled. *I'm right here, being unappreciated!*

I appreciate you, Logan protested.

*You certainly don't **respect** me,* his stallion pointed out. *Right now, you're all caught up in how you're **stuck** like this, how awful it is, how inconvenient it is not to have your fancy fingers and phones. But if I were "just a horse," you'd be caught or lost, because **I'm** the one with access to instinct. If you'd listened to me in the first place, we wouldn't even be in this mess. You take me for granted, and you think that you're better than me just by virtue of being human, but I'm everything that makes you special.*

Logan was completely taken aback, and he stumbled to a stop beside a trickling creek.

His horse was usually self-absorbed and vain, but was Logan himself guilty of exactly the same? His stallion had been his other half for all of his life that he could remember, a constant companion, a second self. But he wasn't *just* a horse. Logan had been around plenty of ordinary animals, and his stallion was not just smarter than any of them, but more complicated...and more connected. His shifter self was a part of himself. They were better together than either of them could be apart.

Maybe it was because of whatever had trapped him in this form that his shifter half had more cognizance now. Or was it that they were closer because of this ordeal, or that Tabby had started to open up his heart to understand his partner's complaint? His horse felt closer, more articulate.

Maybe…

Ooo, oats!

Logan hopped over the creek into the next field and let his stallion graze on the ripening oats that had caught his attention.

Not too much, he cautioned.

His horse snorted. *Says the man who got a stomach ache eating too much buttered popcorn with his niece.*

Maybe they weren't that unalike.

30

Tabby did her chores in the barn and then lingered, as if Logan would somehow miraculously appear in his stall as *Beau* or *Better Behave*, or she might suddenly hear him creaking around in the upstairs apartment. The horses nickered at her and shuffled around. She gave them extra scratches and pats, then went back outside.

His truck was still there, untouched. She went up the stairs and peered into the dark kitchen window.

She was just trying to decide what to do with herself when she heard faint hoofbeats, coming up the drive. She'd left the gate unlocked, still hoping for an Uber carrying Logan, but this was definitely not a car.

There were no lights along the drive, just one at the gate, and one at the house, and all Tabby could see was the dark figure of a horse, trotting tiredly up.

She didn't need to see the white forelock to know who it was, and she went down the stairs two at a time, nearly missing the last one, and bolted out to meet him.

He trotted faster to meet her and came skidding to a

stop as she threw her arms up around his neck. "Logan, Logan, you idiot! Why are you a *horse*?"

He nickered and snuffled at her neck and snorted and hooked her with his head to pull her close.

"Franzi was *frantic*," Tabby lied, because she was the one who'd been a mess. "Why won't you shift?"

Logan blew out in clear frustration.

"Are you *stuck* this way?"

He nodded his big head like a cartoon.

Tabby had to laugh, because she was so relieved to have him back, whether he was a horse or not, and she didn't know what else to do. She leaned against Logan and simply howled, like it was the biggest joke in the world, and maybe it was.

"Oh, Logan. I don't know what to do with you."

But she did, because he was a horse, and he was covered in sweat and moved like he'd been running for two days straight. Tabby knew exactly what he needed.

"You don't get to collapse yet," she scolded him. "I'm putting a cooler on you and you're walking the short track until you cool down. *Slowly.* Nothing faster than a walk. I'll get you fresh water and some hay. No oats. You'll founder."

Tabby had his stall heaped with fresh straw when Logan came obediently back after doing the cooldown laps that she had commanded. He was walking stiffly, but not limping, and his breathing was slower. Tabby verified that his temperature was lower with a hand between his front legs. He hungrily munched at the hay as she rubbed him down.

"What the fresh hell is this?" she said, when she got to his left haunch. There was an angry red mark there, and he flinched when she touched it. "Did someone *brand* you?"

The mark was muddy, she couldn't pick a logo or design out of the burnt flesh, but it was the size and position of a brand—an old-fashioned hot iron brand, not the less painful new freeze-branding kind that was more acceptable now.

"You are mine," she told Logan through gritted teeth as she went for the first aid kit. "I'm going to find the asshole who did this to you and…and…" Tabby wasn't great at threats and had no idea what she would actually do. Something impulsive, probably, and not all that legal.

She cleaned the wound, and although she suspected it was sterile, slathered it with numbing antibiotic cream.

Then she brushed him from nose to tail, untangling his mane and tail and teasing vines and rose brambles out. "You had quite the adventure," she observed, finding a cigarette butt in his tail. Maybe he'd had to hide out in a ditch. Tabby could only imagine how challenging it would be to travel alone as a gorgeous horse like him. He'd probably had to evade several well-meaning rescue attempts. Maybe even some not-so-well-meaning rescue attempts. Montana wasn't free of wild predators, either. All the horrible things she'd tried to keep herself from imagining crowded into her mind and Logan couldn't reassure her they hadn't happened.

"Franzi's sleeping in my guest room," she told him, resting her head against his shoulder, "and I'll take her to day care in the morning, but Logan, I am not cut out to be a single parent and I…I need you back. We gotta figure out how to get you back to two legs, okay? When I said I had no use for you as a man…well, I was wrong about that, okay? Just wrong."

His head snaked around her again and pulled her close, his breath ruffling her hair.

Tabby let herself soak up the comfort he offered before she pushed off of him and dried tears that she didn't realize she'd shed. "I'm going to leave your stall open so you can come and go, okay?"

Logan gave a tired nicker and Tabby checked the straps on the waffle weave cooling blanket. He could get out of it if he wanted to and he looked barely awake enough to keep eating. Tabby made sure his water bucket was topped off and left the stable walking backwards because she wanted to keep him in her sight as long as possible. He'd already disappeared on her as a horse once.

She checked on the other curious horses, assuring them absently that everything was fine, and went back to the house in a daze. Was Logan being stuck shifted only temporary? Would it wear off like a drug? What if he really was a horse forever now? Would the bastard who bought and branded him come looking and find him here? Logan's weak technical loophole didn't actually work if he *couldn't* be a man again, and Tallier had a legal bill of sale for him. Tabby doubted that he'd just let her give the money back and call it done.

She couldn't let him be seen at all, which complicated her boarding and riding lesson business. She'd have to keep him living like a hobo in a back pasture by the fringes of the forest. There was an old run-in shed, but she'd have to see if the roof was still sound.

And what about Franzi? How could she explain taking over guardianship of the little girl while Logan figured out how to get opposable thumbs back?

Tabby froze with her foot above the first step of her porch.

Would *Clancy* get custody of Franzi?

Tabby was badly out of her depth and had no idea what to do. She staggered up the steps and settled into the porch swing.

She couldn't put sweet little Franzi in Clancy

Kennedy's hands. Who even knew what dastardly cons he'd pull with her. No, Tabby had to keep custody of Franzi somehow, and keep Logan hidden from people who came hunting him, no matter that he was a fifteen-hundred pound beast with distinctive markings and…now a *brand*.

Tabby felt her temper sizzle.

Whoever came for either of them, they'd quickly find that Tabitha Swiftwater was not to be trifled with. Let them come. She'd be ready.

31

*L*ogan felt like he'd spent a week on a treadmill without water, sort of dried out, stretched out, and sore. His hip didn't really hurt anymore unless he thought about it, but knowing that the brand was there and feeling the tight place in his skin when he walked made his lips curl back and his teeth grind.

He had thought that coming home might magically allow him to shift again, and he had a moment of hope when he first saw Tabby come running towards him. But try as he might, he could not meet her on two feet and sweep her up into his arms the way he yearned to.

Then he hoped that a night of sleep and resting in a safe place would set things right.

It didn't.

He was still sore, if not as achingly hungry now, and he was still a *horse*.

His stallion was completely unconcerned. *This is comfortable.*

Logan snorted, because he couldn't speak out loud,

and wandered out of his open stall into the morning sunlight.

His muscles were tight, and there was a soreness in his legs that would need working out, but he had run and walked what he guessed was nearly a hundred miles over the past several days, much of it over rough terrain, and he felt pretty good considering.

He missed hands. And speech. And a hundred little human perks he'd always taken for granted.

He walked up to the house and started to climb the porch steps before he realized that there was no way he was going to fit into Tabby's front door.

Fortunately, the door flew open and Franzi came dashing out. "Uncle LOGAN!" Logan lowered his head to meet her and she wrapped her arms around his face. She hugged him, giggling, then backed up. "Why are you a horsey, Uncle Logan? Not SUPOZE to be a horsey. You have to take me to Tiny Paws in the truck!"

Tabby was on Franzi's heels, looking like she was chasing a whirlwind, which maybe she was. She had Franzi's bag and her own purse. "I'm going to have to take you to Tiny Paws, honey. Uncle Logan is having…a little shifting problem, apparently, and we're just going to have to do what we can, okay?"

Logan nodded, which made Franzi giggle, and stepped back, gesturing towards Tabby's truck with his head.

"I can get into Tabby's truck!" Franzi said, though when she tried to, she was unable to reach the door handle. "I can do it! I can do it!" she insisted, when Tabby went to open the door and help her in.

Logan hovered uncomfortably, unable to help at all as Franzi crawled up into the car seat and couldn't get herself buckled in. Tabby got it all sorted with some effort, and Logan wondered when he'd become some kind of expert at it. It didn't seem that long since he'd been struggling with the same exact things.

Of course, with no hands, it was even harder.

"Do you want me to tell the guys at the auto shop that you…ah…can't come in?" Tabby suggested as she shut the truck door on the passenger side.

Logan gave another exaggerated nod.

"Should I tell them you're…sick?"

Logan shook his head emphatically. Sick wouldn't be a logical excuse for a shifter, and Mason would know that. It gave Logan a pang of regret to think that Mason might think he was dodging work. This was the best job he'd ever had and he didn't want to lose it. Again, though, hands were a pretty necessary part of being a mechanic.

"Family emergency?"

Logan sighed and shook his head again. He didn't want to lie to Mason at all, but he didn't know how to tell Tabby that his boss was a shifter and might understand his dilemma. In fact, maybe Mason could figure out a way to help him out, if Tabby told him.

Logan stomped in the dirt and tossed his head.

"I have no idea what that means, Logan," Tabby said in confusion. "You want me to tell him that you had to go out of town for a conference or something?"

Logan blew out in frustration and shook his head. How did you tell someone to *tell the truth* in horse? It was never a problem he'd had before.

"We'll try to set up a whiteboard or something when I get back, okay? They have those toys for animals to train them to ask for things that go terribly wrong with cats, don't they? I'll stop at a pet shop and see if they have one. I have a boarder coming at nine and I need to be back at that time, so I have to go *now*."

She paused long enough to caress his neck and hug his head, kissing the middle of his forehead.

The tingly feeling of her kiss gave Logan a moment of hope. Maybe she'd break his curse with a kiss like a fairy tale!

But if this was a fairy tale, it was one of those old world cautionary tales where little discontented mermaids tragically died on beaches and stepsisters cut off parts of their feet to fit in glass slippers and had their eyes pecked out by ravens.

Her kiss was only a kiss, and then she was getting into the driver's seat and pulling down the driveway with Franzi waving enthusiastically from the passenger seat.

ranzi had a lot to say on the way to Tiny Paws, and she tugged on Tabby's hand as they walked from where she'd parked the truck to make her go faster.

"Push that button!" Franzi commanded when they arrived at the saloon-fronted building.

There was an intercom next to the door and Tabby pushed the call button.

"Tiny Paws Day Care!"

"I'm…ah…dropping off Franzi."

There was a moment of silence over the speaker and the door buzzed. Tabby opened it and Franzi pushed in first. The entryway stretched along the front of the building, separated from the noisy chaos beyond by a tall divider wall with an opening to one side protected by a baby gate. A woman was standing there, eyeing Tabby suspiciously.

"Hello, Franzi," the young woman said carefully, not once looking at the little girl. She had yellow-green eyes, like a cat.

"Hi Teacher Addy! Is Tara here?" Franzi asked,

peeling out of her shoes and leaving them where they dropped. Tabby picked them up, stashed them under the bench with other shoes, and followed Franzi to the gate.

Teacher Addy did not move aside to let them in. "Only Mr. Kennedy is authorized on Franzi's account to drop her off or pick her up."

This was more than just professional caution, Tabby thought, and she remembered that shifters could recognize one another. "I'm not a shifter," she said, deciding honesty was the best choice, and anyway, this was probably already a given. "Logan had a…a…shifting emergency, and I can't keep her today. It's not *safe*." Tabby couldn't risk Clancy coming back and finding Franzi while a client was taking Tabby's time. A terrible thought suddenly occurred to her: if Clancy was looking for Franzi, he might know about Tiny Paws, too. "Franzi has a…relative who might come to try to get her, and she *must not go with him*."

"Is she in *danger*?"

Tabby didn't know how much to say in front of Franzi herself, and when she cast a look at the little girl, who was craning to try to see into the day care, Addy seemed to make up her mind. She stepped to the side and opened the gate.

Tabby realized at the last moment that she was meant to take off her own shoes, and managed to knot the laces of her sneakers trying to get them off too fast, nearly fell down, and finally kicked them under the bench to follow Franzi and Addison into the back.

There were children everywhere, playing various games of pretend and learning motor skills with blocks and soft toys. A woman was changing a baby and tickling it with a feather that appeared to have been shed by an owl chick bouncing nearby. Franzi and Tara were already giggling together in a heap of beanbags, and some of the kids were sitting at a table doing an art project. The middle-aged woman directing these children looked up at their approach with a smile and stood up gracefully from the too-short chair.

"She came in with Franzi," Addy said, giving a barely perceptible shake of her head to the woman. "There might be some kind of *trouble*." They traded subtle little bits of body language that suggested they had worked together for some time, but Tabby wasn't sure what any of it meant.

"I'm Tabby," she introduced herself. "Tabitha Swiftwater. I'm Logan's…landlord." Lover didn't seem appropriate, and they hadn't established anything more.

The woman offered a hand to shake, and Tabby did. She had a solid, gentle grip. "I'm Cherry. I own Tiny Paws. Why don't you come into my office and tell me more."

The office had full-sized chairs, and Tabby gratefully took one as Cherry shut the door, muffling the shrieks and shrill voices from the day care.

"Why don't you tell me what's going on," Cherry suggested, taking a seat across the desk. "Addison said there's trouble?"

Tabby was quiet a moment, trying to gather her thoughts, because she had no idea where to start. "Logan is stuck as a stallion," she said. "He was bought, and branded, and he doesn't seem to be able to shift back. His cousin is probably responsible, and he's not to be trusted with Franzi. Whatever you do, don't let *Clancy Kennedy* take her. He might have another name." It occurred to her that she had a photo of him on her phone from when she was first researching her missing horse, and she started to scroll back to try to find it.

Before she knew what she was doing, Tabby was telling Cherry the entire sordid tale, all out of order, from the Prix to Logan's original sale to her, all about her investigation into the con artists that had probably been the reason that child services finally found Logan. "Here's his photo," she said, when she finally found it. "This is the jerk."

Cherry gave her a phone number to text it to and Tabby did.

"I don't know what we're going to do," Tabby said, knowing she was on the verge of tears and not entirely sure why now when she'd been able to keep it together so far. "Logan can't keep custody as a horse, I'm *nobody* according to the state, and Clancy Kennedy would use her for god *knows* what kinds of awful cons if he got his hands on her."

Cherry listened patiently, occasionally asking for clarification, but didn't seem judgmental about Logan's shady past or questionable life choices. She nodded occasionally, and visibly winced at the idea of a shifter being branded.

"What will you tell Clancy if he comes by demanding custody?" Cherry said, when Tabby had run out of story.

"I thought I'd hide both Logan and Franzi, pretend like Logan had never returned, and tell him that I had handed Franzi back to the state. He can probably figure out that I haven't if he goes looking. I don't know if he'd risk going to CPS directly as himself, but he makes up new identities like they're character sheets in a game. I'm worried he'll just create a new relative to be in order to snap her up. One *without* an arrest warrant. I can't let Franzi go back to foster care, but there's no way they'd just grant me custody out of the blue. I had a friend who did fostering, and it took like a year to get through approvals and background checks."

"We're not going to let Franzi go back to CPS," Cherry said firmly. "And we certainly aren't going to let Clancy Kennedy have her."

"Can *you* take her?" Tabby suggested impulsively. She only realized when she said it that she jealously didn't want to give anyone else Franzi. She'd become desperately fond of the little girl.

"It sounds like she's only just settling in with you and Logan, and I would hate to disrupt that unless we know she's not safe with you," Cherry said firmly. "We don't know for sure that Clancy will come to your ranch looking for her, and I have some contacts that I will get in touch with. The idea of someone selling out shifters is unacceptable to say the least, and there are organizations to protect shifter interests."

Secret organizations for shifters didn't surprise Tabby all that much. If there was magic in the world, why wouldn't there by undercover agencies, too? Maybe even true love..."What about getting Logan back to human form?" Tabby asked, relieved that she wouldn't be losing Franzi immediately. "Do you know how to fix that?"

Cherry shook her head. "I've never heard of that before. But I'll pass the information along and hopefully someone else has some ideas."

Tabby looked at her phone and realized that she was rapidly running out of time. "You have my number. Please let me know if you have any leads at all. I have to be back at my place in twenty minutes, and I still have to get Logan out of work this week, since he can't exactly show up as a horse."

"It was nice to meet you, Tabby," Cherry said, standing to shake her hand again. "Thank you for caring about Franzi."

Tabby wasn't sure why *that* felt like it was going to overflow her eyes, but she blinked back her tears and nodded briskly. "It was nice to meet you," she echoed gruffly.

She stuffed her feet back into the sneakers without tying them in the entry to the day care, nearly killed herself tripping over the laces, and had to stop to unknot them. She opened the day care door to an unwelcome and familiar face.

"Veronica Chase?"

It was an awkward moment where Tabby moved to block her and let the door shut slowly behind her, even as the woman tried to reach for the handle, because she didn't want to accidentally let her into the secretive day care. There was no way to make it look anything less than deliberate or stupid.

"What are you doing here?" Tabby asked, as innocently as possible. Did Veronica know about shifters? Was she still sour about losing the Prix?

"I own the building," Veronica said coldly. "If you'll excuse me?"

To Tabby's relief, the door had fully latched, and Tabby could shrug and pretend that she had nothing to do with it as Veronica smashed the button and demanded to speak with Cherry.

Tabby half-jogged down the street to the auto store where Logan worked.

"I'm looking for Mason," she said to the first technician whose attention she could grab. She was directed to a gruff, burly man taking the lug nuts off an SUV with a wrench that looked too short for the job.

"Mason?"

"Yes, ma'am?"

"I wanted to let you know that due to circumstances outside of his control, Logan wouldn't be coming in to work today." Tabby had gone over all the stories she could come up with and decided that vague truth was the best idea.

Mason was quiet, still crouched by the SUV. "I suppose there is a reason he didn't call and tell me that himself?"

"Yes, there is," Tabby said unhelpfully. "And I don't

know when he'll be able to come back in, but please give him a chance. He's a good guy, and he deserves this job. This isn't…his fault."

Mason's mouth worked, like he was trying to decide what to make of Tabby's plea.

"I…appreciate the update," he finally said mildly. "His voicemail was full."

Tabby gave him her own number, fretting at the time it took for him to wipe off his hands so he could handle his phone, and then sprinted back to where her truck was parked. There was a parking ticket on her windshield like a sprinkle of bad luck, and Tabby threw it into Franzi's car seat with a few select words.

She barely avoided getting a speeding ticket to add to it, and arrived at her ranch to find her boarding client waiting at the locked gate.

Fortunately, they had not been waiting long, and Tabby was glad to have work to keep her busy. Logan's stall was empty and there was no sign of the stallion, which was a relief. She gave the client a brief tour, signed paperwork with them, and got their horse—a smallish dun mare with a lively step that suggested she would be a joy to ride —settled.

She locked the gate again after they left.

33

*L*ogan had always taken a certain amount of visceral pleasure from being a horse. He loved the strength and speed he had in this form, and, shallowly, the way he was admired. He got plenty of second glances as a man, but as a horse, he got outright admiration.

Now, he would have given anything to have his own body back.

He spent the time that Tabby was gone wandering the ranch and trying everything he could think of to shift back.

He'd never dwelled much on *how* shifting worked, or analyzed what he did when he switched forms. It was like snapping or whistling; once he'd learned the trick to it, he never looked back. All he had to do was imagine himself as the form he wasn't, and flow into that shape instinctually.

With plenty of time to kill and absolutely nothing he was otherwise capable of doing, he ruminated over the mechanics of magic.

***Cows** are the ones who ruminate*, his stallion reminded him in disgust. *We don't have second stomachs.*

It's an expression, Logan replied shortly.

Well, it's foolish, and you're thinking too much, the horse complained. *It's a sunny day and our hide is warm. It smells good and we have the run of the ranch.*

We have to figure a way out of this, Logan insisted. *I'm not staying a horse forever.*

Is it that bad? his stallion demanded. *What's wrong with being a horse?*

Everything!

The sound of a vehicle and the distinctive rattle of a trailer at the gate sent Logan trotting off to the woods above Tabby's house. He waited there, shrouded in shrubs, and watched as Tabby's truck came around the bend in the driveway not long afterwards, leading a strange truck with a horse trailer to the stable.

Tabby talked with two people for some time, signed some papers on the hood of her truck, and led a dun mare into the stable. Hands were shaken, hats were tipped, and the strangers drove away. Tabby walked after them, probably to lock the gate, and Logan came to meet her as she came back, his ears pricked for other interlopers.

"I was hoping you'd be human when I got back," Tabby admitted, greeting Logan with an embrace and a pat. "I told Mason you couldn't come in, but I didn't tell him why, or how long you'd be gone. I don't know how long you'll have a job, but I *tried*. I met Addison and Cherry, and Cherry says she knows some people. There's an agency that protects shifters, but she was pretty vague, and I'm not sure if she doesn't know more, or if she just wasn't telling me because I'm not a shifter."

Logan snorted conversationally.

"I didn't have time to stop at a pet store for one of those communication pads, but I saw a felt board on an easel with letters in Franzi's room. I could bring that out."

Logan followed her to the stable and waited at the bottom of the stairs as she walked up to his apartment with two easy legs and her spare key. At least she was still fun to watch, even if he couldn't follow her up the stairs.

She came back out with the board. Even with Tabby to lay the letters out on the porch and stick them to the board, it was painfully laborious to pick out individual letters. T-H-I-S S-U-C-K-5, Logan spelled, using a five when he ran out of esses.

Tabby laughed half-hysterically and patted his neck.

Now that he was faced with the board, he wasn't sure what to spell out. He wanted to tell Tabby everything, but he didn't have room or dexterity to summarize the important bits of his story, and there were only two esses.

"Who branded you?" Tabby demanded. "Did Clancy do this?"

T-A-L-L-I-E-R, he spelled.

"Taller? Oh, wait, Tallier?" Tabby looked at it in confusion. "Someone named Tallier branded you? Was Tallier your buyer?"

Logan bobbed his head up and down.

"You're going to have to be careful, Logan," Tabby told him unnecessarily. "I have boarders coming and going, and I don't want word to get back to him that you're here."

F-R-A-N— He didn't have to finish the word.

"I will take care of her," Tabby swore. "I'm not going to let Clancy get her. Or child services. Or Tallier, whoever the hell he is. That little girl needs a home, *this* home, and I will protect her when you can't."

Logan's heart swelled up inside his chest. Tabby *knew*. She knew how much he'd come to care about Franzi, and she was capable and smart. His niece was safe with her, however long this inconvenient curse went on, and it was both a relief and a surprise. He'd never had anyone to trust before.

Except for ME, his stallion reminded him, huffy. *Hello, am I chopped river?*

Chopped liver, Logan corrected. *It's an—*

—Expression. I KNOW.

C-L-A—

"Clancy," Tabby guessed. "Did Clancy have something to do with this? Did he sell you out and not just *sell* you?"

Logan nodded, but slowly, and finished it with rocking his head side-to-side. Horse shoulders weren't designed for shrugs.

"Maybe? You're not sure?"

Logan nodded more clearly.

"Are you worried that he'll want to take Franzi?"

This nod was vigorous.

"I warned them at Tiny Paws," Tabby said fiercely. "I made sure that they know not to give her to him for any reason."

Of course she had; she was as brilliant as she was beautiful.

"How did you get stuck?" Tabby wanted to know next. "More importantly, how do we fix this?"

Logan looked back at his flank. He wasn't positive that the brand was the reason for his predicament, but he was pretty sure it was at least related.

"Does it have to do with the brand?" Tabby guessed.

Logan gave another nod-shake.

"Do you know how to fix it?" Tabby asked.

Logan gave a definite head-shake. He had no idea. Nothing he had tried seemed to do anything.

You're just wrong, his stallion complained, but he couldn't say *how.* Being stuck as a horse didn't seem to bother him as much as the fact that Logan himself was off-kilter.

Tabby gave a deep sigh. "I'm going to go make sure the new girl is settling in, and then why don't you and I go for a ride? I need to exercise Trudy and train with Oreo, and you shouldn't have a completely sedentary day after the journey you've had. How far did you go?"

They tried for a few futile moments to figure out how to show her on a map on her phone, but Logan frankly had only the faintest idea where he'd been, instinct hadn't given him any street names, and the screen was hard to see, being barely bigger than one of his horse nostrils. He could only look at it with one eye at a time.

Tabby adjusted her hat and rested her hand on his nose. "Don't worry," she said kindly. "We'll figure something out."

The ride was unexpectedly pleasant, and Tabby wasn't wrong; it felt good to stretch his legs again as they took one of the longer trails, and Logan knew that it was smart not to have a rider for the leisurely trip. Trudy started out shying at blowing leaves and balking at places where the trail was overgrown, but Logan bumped her hip with his head and she settled, automatically responding to his stallion's protective presence.

At the end of their route, Tabby took Trudy through a short, easy jumping course. The horse clearly loved to leap and tried to take the course again. Logan whinnied at her and she sighed and let Tabby dismount.

"You're a good influence," Tabby said to Logan, as she settled the mare into her stall with fresh water and hay. "She liked having you along for that ride."

Logan followed her around to her other chores like he was Franzi, desperate to stay close to her. She smelled like…

Hay, his stallion supplied.

Hope, Logan countered.

When Tabby was finished with her chores, she stood in the middle of the yard and hugged Logan hard. He'd never longed so deeply to have arms to hug her back with.

"I love you, Logan," she murmured into his chest.

Logan froze.

They hadn't spoken of love before, or talked about what kind of relationship they really had, because Logan hadn't wanted to think too hard about it. She'd been so adamant that their relationship wasn't a romance, down-playing any definition of their partnership.

Mate, his stallion said in satisfaction, nuzzling Tabby when Logan wasn't sure what to do. *Herd.*

Tabby was everything he'd ever wanted in a woman or a partner. She was soft, strong, and honest. She set him on fire and kept him from burning out, all at once. Logan had never met anyone so kind and capable. He adored her humor, her impulsiveness, and her work ethic.

But he didn't deserve her love.

He was a trainwreck in a three-quarter-ton horse. He had more baggage than a tourist, and if it weren't for Franzi, he'd have left her high and dry months ago, because…that's what he did. The stability and safety he'd found at her ranch and in her arms was not in his nature. He'd spent his entire life running and changing his identity, living in the moment, and leaving whenever things got too intense. As much as he felt at home here at last, he was still waiting for the other boot to drop, sure that the beautiful fantasy he'd been living would inevitably be snatched away.

You're overthinking this, his stallion snorted. *She is our mate, this is our herd.*

But Tabby deserved someone whole and secure, someone who could love her back with his whole heart.

Someone who wasn't just pretending at parenting, someone who was actually capable of living this life.

Someone who wasn't just a horse.

34

Franzi was very, *very* quiet as she and Tabby packed up all of her things into her suitcases to move her into Tabby's house that afternoon.

Tabby had no idea how long Logan was going to be in horse-limbo, and she wanted Franzi in the house with her, not sleeping across the yard and up a flight of stairs. She considered moving into Logan's bedroom, but knew it would be too lonely without him, and the apartment was inconveniently small and all of her own things were in her house; it seemed infinitely simpler to move Franzi in with her rather than the other way around.

But Tabby second guessed that decision when she saw how uncertain and unsettled Franzi was, and how unnaturally silent she got. Tabby hadn't realized how constantly she talked until she wasn't saying a word.

"It's your very own horsey room," Tabby said. She'd moved the more valuable models up high out of reach, and left enough down to play with that she thought Franzi would be entertained. Her wooden rocking horse, sanded safe but not yet finished, was in one corner and Tabby had emptied the desk for her to use.

Did this make Franzi think of moving around through the foster care system? Did she believe that she was going to be abandoned again?

"Are you okay, Franzi? You know that Uncle Logan loves you and he isn't going to leave, right?"

Franzi was holding a stuffy and she pressed her face down into it.

Tabby's heart gave a twang. "I'm not going to leave, either," she promised, sitting down on the edge of Franzi's bed. "Even if Uncle Logan stays a horsey forever, you've got me, okay?" To her surprise, she meant it. If she'd fallen hard for Logan, she'd fallen even harder for Franzi, who was sweet and stubborn and fragile and needed love more than air.

Franzi squeezed her stuffy harder and didn't say a word.

Why was this so impossible? Tabby didn't have the right words to comfort her and it only made her realize her own despair. "I miss him as a human, too," she said sadly. "At least we still have him as a horse."

Franzi's head suddenly popped up and swiveled towards the window, just as Tabby realized she was hearing a car in the drive. She wasn't expecting anyone, and for a moment she was cross, and then she was alarmed. Was it someone coming looking for Logan?

"Stay here, sweetheart," she told Franzi. "Shut the door and don't let anyone in, okay? Promise you'll stay here?"

She didn't want Franzi to watch them haul Logan away if they caught him, and she hoped that Logan had enough sense to be somewhere else when he heard the car coming in.

It was, at least, just a car, not a truck with a trailer, but Tabby's moment of relief was short-lived. Clancy Kennedy got out of the SUV.

"Ms. Swiftwater!" he called, as he rounded the fancy black vehicle. Two big goons got out with him, one from the passenger seat, and one from behind.

"Can I help you?" Tabby knew she sounded hostile and didn't care. Was it Clancy's fault that Logan was trapped as a horse? Logan was nowhere to be seen, and she desperately hoped that he'd seen Clancy coming and hidden himself.

Tabby noticed at once that Clancy was doing a masterful job of looking around without *looking* like he was looking around, and she remembered Logan's laughing lessons on subterfuge. It was a lot less funny with Clancy than it was with Logan.

"Is Logan around? I thought we might drink to a successful transaction!" Clancy raised a bottle of wine.

As if it was perfectly normal to bring bodyguard goons to a business toast. Were they there to guard Clancy or to keep him in line?

Tabby crossed her arms in front of herself. "The bastard skipped out on me!" she said at the spur of the moment. "Never came back, left me high and dry with months of back rent due!"

If she hadn't been watching carefully for it, she wouldn't have seen the flash of delight in Clancy's face. Tabby might not have magical instinct, but she was a good read of character, and she could tell that Clancy had *not* been coming to celebrate with Logan.

Clancy quickly masked his reaction with a look of shock. "He didn't! What about that sweet niece of ours?"

Tabby wanted to reach for the dinner bell clanger hanging on her porch and clock him over the head. "I wasn't going to keep the kid," she scoffed. "Logan Kennedy wasn't paying me enough to be a nanny. Child services came and got her yesterday."

Clancy's eyes flashed briefly in anger and Tabby's resolve hardened. There was no way she was letting him get his mitts on Franzi.

"You don't mind if we look around, do you?"

"Let me give you a tour," Tabby said acidly, mindful of Logan's advice to always stay in control of the situation. "You can take the deadbeat's stuff with you and save me the refuse fees."

The apartment was so sparsely furnished and Logan had so few possessions that it was believable he would skip out in that state. Tabby opened the refrigerator door to point out the food that had been left there since before the championship. "You're welcome to take the science experiments with you," she said.

Franzi's room was stripped. None of her toys or clothing remained behind, and Tabby pulled out the empty drawers to make a point. She had no regrets now that she'd moved the little girl into the house, and she hoped as hard as she could that Franzi wouldn't get bored and come out. Would instinct keep her hidden? Her understanding of instinct was vague at best, but Logan had said he thought it was stronger in younger shifters to keep them safe.

Right now, it might be the only thing keeping her safe.

They went down to the barn after that, and Tabby was not surprised that they peered in every stall. Her boarders greeted the visitors according to their personality, begging for treats or staying snottily out of reach. It was clear that Logan was not here. One of the big men went and poked into the hay, as if he might be hiding underneath it.

"That's Logan's bike," Clancy observed, looking into one of the stalls.

"I plan to sell that to recoup some of the rent he owes me," Tabby said flippantly. She'd forgotten it was there; Logan hadn't worked on it since they parked it there the day he moved in. "His truck, too."

"Satisfied?" Tabby asked, when they had gone through the big barn and she had opened the garden shed to prove that Logan couldn't possibly be in there. They didn't ask to come in the house, as if Clancy *knew* that he wouldn't be there as a man, and Tabby was deeply relieved; Clancy's flash of anger when he thought Tabby had sent Franzi away suggested that the little girl had been his ultimate goal. She had no idea where Logan actually was, but she was glad he had the sense to stay away. "If you find that bastard, you *call* me, because he owes me a lot more than money."

They would assume she was a jilted lover, Tabby realized as she heard her own words. That was probably in character for Logan, and he'd said that the best way to do a con was to play to your strengths. So she channeled all her leftover anger about her ex-husband and hoped she looked properly betrayed. Mostly, she was surprised to discover how *little* she cared about Hank any more.

Clancy was all smoothness and charm again as they went back to his car and his goons got in. "I hope you won't hold any of this against me, Ms. Swiftwater," he said, offering to shake her hand and then fawning over it. "I genuinely thought that we'd be setting things right. I had no idea that Logan would leave us high and dry like this."

"Call me if you track him down," Tabby said loftily, taking her hand back. She looked beyond him towards the house and realized that Franzi's car seat was in plain view in the passenger seat of her truck. There was absolutely no reason to have Franzi's car seat still if she *had* given the girl over to child services.

Tabby hoped her face hadn't done anything awful at the realization and scowled.

"We'll be in touch," Clancy promised. If he suspected anything, he didn't give any indication, and Tabby was glad to see the last of his SUV. She walked to the end of the drive behind him to close the gate, noticing a second vehicle with a horse trailer down the highway that might have been waiting along the road. She locked the gate.

Then she turned and sprinted back to the house, bursting into Franzi's room with a frantic, "Franzi, honey, are you okay?"

All of the model horses had been spread out on the floor, and several fell over when Tabby opened the door. Franzi, looking guilty, was sitting in the middle of them holding the two most expensive. "I was playing," she said angelically.

"How did you get those down?" Tabby choked, willing her heart to stop thumping so hard.

"I climbed," Franzi said with a hopeful smile. "Am I in trouble?"

Tabby moved two horses and lowered herself down to the floor very slowly and carefully. "No, honey," she said in relief. "You're not in trouble. You're home."

35

It took all of Logan's self-control and serenity to stay in the shelter of the forest looking out at Tabby's ranch. Clancy's SUV was there for far too long, and Logan didn't have to smell the greasy men with him to know that they reeked of Tallier's money. Clancy was deeper in this than Logan understood. How else would Tallier have known who and what Logan really was? Was Clancy responsible for the brand, too?

He lay in the brush until the truck was long gone, and then waited until after twilight had crept into true night before he stood, shook himself, and trotted down to Tabby's house.

Franzi came flying out to greet him. "I have a horsey room!" she exclaimed. For a joyful moment, Logan thought he would be able to scoop her up into two arms, but his legs remained horse legs and he had to settle for letting her hug his face and nickering happily.

"Thank *heavens*," Tabby said warmly, coming out behind Franzi. "I'm guessing you saw our very unwelcome visitor?"

Logan bobbed his head and snorted.

Franzi babbled about her day and Tabby leaned against his side and buried her face in his mane.

Finally, she sighed. "Franzi, honey, I need you to get ready for bed. If you're ready to tuck in within ten minutes, we can sit out on the porch and I'll read you and Uncle Logan a story, okay?"

"Okay!" Franzi tripped back inside. Logan wanted to warn Tabby about all the ways leaving her alone in the bathroom could go wrong, but was thwarted by his horse tongue in its horse mouth.

"Your lessons in lying were useful," Tabby said, coming to stroke his neck. "I think they believed me when I said I sent Franzi packing and was planning to sell your stuff to cover back rent."

He'll be back, Logan wanted to warn her.

"If Clancy goes to child services, they'd probably tell him that she's still here," Tabby cautioned. "He might come back. CPS might come looking for her. We should find a safe place to send her. But I don't know where that would be. And there was a warrant out for him in California; he might not risk going to state services." She rubbed her face. "You know, my friends used to make fun of me for talking to horses like they were people." Tabby leaned her head against his shoulder and stroked his neck. "I miss you, Logan," she said. "Human you, I mean. You're a great horse, and I love you both ways, but human you was a much better conversationalist."

Logan snaked his head around to press against her shoulder and they stood that way until Tabby relaxed a little against him.

She was so strong and smart. How did he deserve her trust and loyalty?

She is our mare, his stallion said matter-of-factly. *Our mate. She completes our herd.*

I love her, Logan replied in wonder. It was so unfair that he couldn't tell her now. Frustration made him snort against Tabby's neck, and she gave a tired giggle.

"I'd better go see what's keeping Franzi," she said, giving Logan one final pat and stepping back away from him.

Logan leaned his head on the porch rail and watched her go inside.

I love her.

His stallion didn't seem to find this as much of a revelation as he did. *Why does it surprise you to care about her?*

I've never trusted anyone enough to care about them, Logan realized. But Franzi trusted *him*, and he couldn't help but love her…and that let him love Tabby, too.

He wished that he could tell Tabby that, even more desperately than he wished he had hands.

36

Tabby opened her eyes in the dead of the night and lay in the darkness listening sleepily for Franzi.

The little girl didn't cry often when she was awake, but every once in a while she'd give a wail of alarm as she woke.

There were crickets outside, and Tabby wasn't sure at first what had disturbed her sleep. Then she recognized the sound of crunching gravel, like someone was trying to walk quietly. For a moment she thought it was Logan wandering around outside, but then there was a creak of floorboards that she recognized as the sound of someone walking on the porch.

Oh, *hell* no.

Tabby was wide awake now, and she groped for the length of pipe that she kept beside her bed.

Clancy? The mysterious Tallier? An unrelated thief who thought her ranch looked like easy pickings?

Tabby paused long enough to yank on her jeans but

remained barefoot and wore only a T-shirt on top. Her arms goosebumped in the chilly night air as she tiptoed out. Someone was testing the windows from the porch and she closed her grip harder on the pipe.

Should she open the door and confront them, or wait for them to break in? Tabby's heart raced, her throat was tight, and she couldn't breathe deep enough to get air to think. Her palms were sweaty on the slick pipe and her jaw was clenched.

It felt like that moment when she knew she'd been thrown from a horse but hadn't hit the ground yet, knowing it was going to hurt but not sure how bad—but stretched out into infinity. They scratched quietly at the lock and she just got more and more wound up.

Call someone! Of course she should *call someone,* Tabby realized. Did she have time now? Would it give her precious element of surprise away? Where was her phone?

She'd left it charging on the kitchen counter, she remembered, because she hated having the distraction of it in the bedroom with her at night. She backed out of the living room, glad to have something to do but worried she'd wasted too much time already. Her hammering heart was hard to think around.

If it was someone here to take Franzi, was Tabby strong enough to stop them? Did they have a *gun?* It was a risky thing to break into a farmhouse in Montana, as well-armed as the population tended to be. It was a cowboy state, and most people could shoot tin cans off of fences by the time they were sixteen. Tabby could, but she'd never been terribly comfortable with weapons, and she didn't have anything suitable for protection against home invasion.

The person on the porch had given up on the windows and was making *snick-snick* noises at the deadbolt like they were trying to pick it. They were trying to sneak in now, but did that mean they didn't have backup?

The kitchen was darker than the living room, which at least had the nightlight from the bathroom to cast a little light, and Tabby tripped over a stuffy and took the edge of the island in her side. She froze, listening, and at that moment, the deadbolt at the front door shot back with its distinctive thunk.

Tabby stayed still, not daring to go for her phone. Maybe the intruder wouldn't see her. She wished she had a better grip on her pipe, and her fingers were already aching from clenching on it so hard.

The door opened without hesitation, and as Tabby wavered between charging forward with her pipe or hiding, the lights flipped on.

"Good evening, Tabby Swiftwater," Clancy Kennedy said smoothly, as if he hadn't just broken into her house. "You're a terrible liar, do you know that?"

He *did* have a gun—a wicked-looking revolver—and he was pointing it straight at her.

"What do you think I lied about?" Tabby bluffed. "Logan never came back."

"Logan had outlived his usefulness anyway. I'm here for my darling niece."

"I told you—"

"Yes, it was a very convincing story about child services taking her, and it was a useful show in getting Tallier's men off my back. But I did have to pay him back in full what he paid for Logan with interest, and I still need to recoup those losses. Franzi is young enough to be molded into a better partner than he ever was."

Tabby's terror was swamped with outrage and she lifted her pipe. "Don't you lay a finger on that girl."

Clancy smiled. "I like you, Tabby. You've got moxie.

But I have a gun, and Franzi's *my blood*. A court would probably back me up on this, and I'm not leaving without her." He sounded so calm and reasonable.

Tabby's brain seemed to be in overdrive, to make up for her previous numbness. Could she get him to put the gun down? Picking up Franzi, maybe? Could she fool him into thinking that she would give up that little girl without a fight? Even if he didn't have a gun, did she have a chance to subdue him physically?

She had to outthink him somehow. For once, she was glad that all of her terror was transparent on her face and she lowered her pipe reluctantly, like she was reconsidering her position.

"Atta girl," Clancy said, like she was a stubborn horse to soothe. "Put it down on the floor. You know that you can't stop me. Now go get Franzi for me."

"She's only four," Tabby pleaded, putting the pipe down. It wouldn't do much good against bullets. Her phone was there on the counter between boxes of cereal and the coffee maker. Could she get to it and call 9-1-1? Clancy still had the gun trained on her. "Doesn't she deserve a safe home like *this*? Please leave her with me."

"You do realize that you're the reason that I need her, don't you?" Clancy said, in his too-reasonable voice.

"*Me?*" Tabby was genuinely confused.

"Your harmless little investigation into my cousin and I led to a whole lot of *private* information becoming *public*. The cops got my other identities and put heat on my best forgers. It's been hard to make an honest living with them on my tail." His voice took an angry edge.

Tabby told herself not to scoff at the idea of Clancy pursuing an *honest living*.

"I had no idea that it would cause you problems," she

said humbly. "But Franzi would still be better off with me. You know that. Don't you want the best for her?" Did Clancy have a soft side to appeal to like Logan had proved to have?

"That's so sweet," Clancy said in a hard voice. "I'm looking out for one person now, and that's me." He waggled the tip of the gun at her. "Now, if you'll get the girl, we'll be on our way."

Tabby tried again, "You know it's not right. I would be—"

"Get the brat, or I will."

Did she risk getting shot and fight him at every step, or did she play along? Tabby reminded herself to *breathe* so she could think.

She padded, still barefoot, to Franzi's room and cracked the door open, keenly aware of Clancy in the hallway behind her.

Franzi was asleep, sprawled almost sideways across the bed as if she'd fallen asleep in the middle of a cartwheel. The blankets were half on her, half hanging off the bed.

"You have to wake up, Franzi."

Franzi squirmed and came awake. Her trusting eyes were big and bright.

"Your Uncle Logan's cousin, Clancy, is here to—" It broke Tabby's heart to say the rest. "—take you away."

But Franzi didn't protest the move, or the fact that it was the middle of the night. She only slid bonelessly out of bed and went to the closet for her suitcases.

Clancy watched them from the doorway, always alert. Tabby used the tricks Logan had taught her about keeping an eye on him without seeming to and he never relaxed, even when Franzi was completely dressed, with a jacket right over her pajamas, and her bags were packed.

Franzi didn't say a word the whole time, but Tabby's heart melted and her will hardened at the girl's brave front. No four-year-old should *ever* have to go through this.

"Get her in the car," Clancy said, stepping back to give them room.

"You'll need her car seat," Tabby said, still casting for some way to stop this all from happening. "They'll do traffic stops for that."

"Fine," Clancy said in frustration.

"And keep her in the back seat," Tabby added. "It's much safer there."

"I don't need a safety lecture," Clancy said dismissively. "Get moving."

Tabby took Franzi's suitcases. The little girl walked so close to Tabby that she banged against them.

"Hang on," Tabby said impulsively as they came out into the living room. She put the suitcases down.

"What are you doing?"

Tabby wasn't sure if it was that she had hit some new level of adrenaline exhaustion or if the terror of Clancy's gun was starting to lose its sharp edge. "I'm getting her a granola bar for the road," she said boldly. "She needs some food."

Clancy looked like he wanted to argue, but he blew out instead. "Fine. But don't go any closer to that phone. Don't think I didn't notice it there."

"I won't," Tabby promised, yanking open the junk drawer. There was a granola bar right on top, but she made a show of searching for it, sifting through the lighters and twist-ties and chip clips until she found what she was really looking for. "Here." She held up the granola bar, palming the luggage tag beneath it. If she could find a safe place on Franzi to tuck it, she could follow them wherever they went. Maybe she could get it under the cushion of the car seat.

Having some kind of backup plan helped settle her and Tabby's knees weren't shaking quite so badly while she pulled on her shoes without socks, Clancy trying to hurry everything along.

Logan was waiting there in the dark by Clancy's car.

He was a great hulking shape in the silky midnight Montana air, and he snorted and pawed the gravel.

"Never came back?" Clancy sneered, shoving Tabby and Franzi down the porch steps ahead of him. "Why cousin, shouldn't you shift to say hello?" Tabby had no doubt from his tone that he knew Logan couldn't shift.

"He's got a gun," Tabby called to Logan in warning, even though Logan could probably see in the dark better than she could, being a horse. She didn't want him to do something stupid like charge Clancy and get shot. Logan pretended he was cold and calculating, but he had a huge streak of nobility, and he adored Franzi.

"Yes, I've got a gun," Clancy said. "And I'm going to take my niece and you're going to let us go, because you know what's good for you."

"She's not actually your niece," Tabby corrected him. "She would be your second cousin, once removed. Or maybe first cousin, once removed. I'm not entirely sure."

"Get her in the car," Clancy said impatiently.

But Logan, moving like dark water, came between Tabby and the car.

"Don't do anything stupid, Logan," she begged softly.

"Listen to your girlfriend," Clancy said, and he was close now. Close enough that Tabby could feel the cold weight of the end of the gun when he rested it on her skull. Her fear of the gun returned with a vengeance and Tabby felt like her heart was going to pound out of her chest.

"You don't need the brat," Clancy said smoothly.

"She's just dead weight to you anyway. I take her, and we go our separate ways forever. We'll be even this way."

Logan snorted and Tabby could see his hide shiver.

"I need to get the car seat," Tabby said carefully, setting the suitcases down in the gravel. "Franzi can't go without it."

Franzi was still silent, clinging to Tabby's arm and Tabby started to take her with her towards the truck.

"I'll come with you," Clancy said suspiciously, and it was an awkward shuffle across the driveway, Franzi like a little barnacle, Clancy close beside with the gun on Tabby, and Logan gliding after them like a ghost horse.

Tabby got to the truck door. "It's locked," she realized. "I'll have to go in and get my keys."

"Forget the car seat," Clancy snarled. "You're just wasting my time now." Logan's presence seemed to set him on edge.

Logan, on the other hand, gave a nicker like a laugh.

"Get back," Clancy growled, and Logan stepped back slowly.

It was two against one now, Tabby realized, and Logan was a whole *lot* of horse. Clancy seemed unsettled by his presence.

She just had to get the gun away from him somehow, without putting Franzi in any danger, and that was challenging with Franzi still clinging to her.

Clancy dragged them back to his own car over Tabby's half-hearted protests about the car seat, and opened the back door. "Get in, kid."

Franzi began to cry and fold into herself unhappily, in the classic trick that Tabby had now witnessed several times where suddenly her legs didn't work. Tabby pretended not to expect it and let herself be dragged down with the little girl.

Clancy, who had one hand clamped around her arm, stooped down after her, the gun wavering from Tabby's head at last.

And in that moment, Logan struck.

37

*L*ogan knew he had a whole lot of unresolved anger and emotional baggage to work through, and he was pretty sure that pounding Clancy into a bloody pulp would solve a lot of it.

Clancy was shifter fast, and he recognized what was happening exactly as Logan reared up and struck out with his front feet. Logan was handicapped for just a moment with worry for Tabby and Franzi, and he was glad when Tabby dived over the little girl and pulled her into the insufficient cover of the open car door, just as a single shot rang out. He didn't have time to figure out if one of them had been shot and could only hope he hadn't screwed this up, too.

The gun, Logan's first priority, went skittering out of Clancy's grip when he was clipped by Logan's hoof, and the car took the brunt of Logan's charge as Clancy slithered away. Tabby was hauling Franzi into the car and out of the way, and now the fight was an unarmed man versus a pissed off horse.

Logan didn't wait for Clancy to collect himself or draw

a blade to defend himself with, but attacked furiously, plunging and using his entire body as a weapon. He struck Clancy several glancing blows that he barely twisted away from.

"Cousin!" Clancy cried desperately. "I didn't sell you out!"

Logan didn't believe him and didn't pause in his assault. Clancy's first defense was always the lie that he thought someone wanted to hear. He'd threatened Tabby and taken Franzi, and that was enough reason for Logan.

He is not our herd, his stallion agreed. *Drive him away.*

Clancy must have guessed that his silver tongue was going to get him nowhere, and he turned away in time to shift and kick back to catch Logan in the chest with one rear hoof.

Slowed, but not badly hurt, Logan engaged again, this time clashing legs with Clancy as he spun and reared to meet the attack. Clancy's head snaked forward to bite at Logan's neck, and Logan used his longer neck to bite back more successfully.

Clancy might be more horse than he was man, but his horse was smaller than Logan's, and less fit. Logan had been training hard with Tabby, and working even harder at the auto shop; he was in the best shape of his life, and he had everything to lose. He could turn faster and rear higher, and Clancy screamed as Logan battered at him with hard hooves, getting hit after hit through his flailing legs at his chest and flank.

Clancy tried to flee, but Logan was faster, and far more determined.

"Stop!" A gunshot cracked in the air.

Tabby, brave, clever Tabby, had closed the car door on Franzi and found the gun, and she was pointing it in the air rather than trying to train a shot on one of them in their tangled battle.

Logan paused and Clancy backed away. They faced each other, sides heaving.

Logan had several bad scrapes and his head was ringing from a lucky kick, but he thought he'd gotten more hits on Clancy than he'd taken himself. It was hard to tell, in the dark, how badly either of them was hurt.

Would Clancy back down or continue the fight, now that Tabby had the most dangerous weapon?

Do something dumb, he dared Clancy in his own head.

And Clancy did.

38

abby had forgotten that Clancy was a horse shifter too, until he turned into a big rough-coated buckskin and fought Logan in earnest.

For one awful moment after she dove, she was sure that she'd done a dumb thing and was going to get herself—or Logan!—shot when she went down with Franzi, but when she could hear again after the round went off near her ear, none of them appeared to have been injured.

Her first priority was getting Franzi as safe as she could get her, tucked into the back seat footwell of Clancy's car. She tucked the luggage tag under the mat and closed the door, then went cursing out into the darkness to try to find the gun. The car was struck several times during the horse battle, and Tabby had to dodge flailing limbs. It was sheer dumb luck that she heard her foot hit the gun and scrape it on the gravel over the sound of the stallions squealing and clashing with each other.

It was a heavy gun, and double action, and it made a satisfying crack as she stopped the battle with it.

But Tabby's moment of triumph was short-lived, because Clancy, presumably thinking she wouldn't dare fire at him, turned away from his standoff with Logan and charged *her*.

Was he planning to shift and tear the gun away from her, knowing it was the only way to stop Logan? Did he think he could simply bowl her over and remove the threat?

Tabby aimed the gun and almost squeezed the trigger, but Logan was on a split-second intercept course, and she didn't dare in case he was too close.

Instead of hitting her, Clancy hit the car with all of Logan's weight driving into him and it rocked in place as Franzi screamed from inside.

Clancy went down with an alarming *crunch*, and Logan gave a bird-of-prey screech and reared over him, clearly intent on trampling him into the ground.

"Don't!" Tabby cautioned. "Don't kill him!" Would Clancy be human when the cops came? How would she explain *either* of them as a corpse?

Logan's wicked hooves came down in the gravel so close to Clancy that he probably shaved horse hair off of his cousin's legs.

Shaking, willing her own legs to keep holding her up, Tabby went to train the gun on Clancy. "Shift, you sonuvabitch."

Clancy did, both of his hands spread before him in defeat. One of his legs was crumpled awkwardly beneath him.

"Did you break your leg?" Tabby asked. "Because I'm *happy* to put you down."

Logan snorted. Tabby wasn't sure if it was rebuke or agreement.

Clancy crawled to his feet, though he limped and looked worse for the wear even in the poor light. "What are you going to do?" he challenged, spitting something to the ground. Tabby hoped it was a tooth. Inside the car, Franzi was wailing.

"I could call the cops," Tabby said, trying to keep her hands steady. She wasn't sure that she actually had the guts to shoot Clancy. Then she remembered that he'd come to steal Franzi, and her resolve hardened. "But there's another agency that can do more good. An agency that keeps shifters in check. They don't appreciate the fact that you're selling out shifter secrets for your own gain."

"I'm not afraid of…"

"You should be," Tabby said ferociously. "You should be really afraid. You just broke into *my* house and stole *my* kid at gunpoint."

"Let me go," Clancy countered, suddenly sounding dangerously reasonable again. "You've won and all I'm asking for is a head start. Keep Logan. Keep the brat. Just let me leave."

"How do I know you won't turn around and come right back?" Tabby asked.

"You have my wor—"

"Your word is worthless," Tabby reminded him. "But here's what you need to remember. You conned me, and I *found* you. The only motivation I had then was a missing horse that I'd had less than a day. This time, you've threatened my ranch and my *family.* If you come here and try to take them again, there is no stone I won't turn over. There is nowhere in the world you can take these two that I won't follow you and *take them back.* You leave here now, and you go to ground, and you *stay there*, because if I so much as get a whiff of your ugly stink, I will hunt you down and destroy you for good." The weight of the gun in her hand was a comfort, but not as much of a comfort as Logan, who stomped behind her. She wasn't sure that the horse *agreed* with her decision, but he'd back her up.

And she didn't know what else to do. She couldn't hold Clancy at gunpoint forever. Who even knew when the cops could get there, if she could call them, and the mysterious shifter agency would probably take even longer. She wasn't on record as Franzi's guardian, so the police would never let Tabby keep her, and Logan was still a horse.

She edged to the side and opened the back door of Clancy's car, keeping the gun trained on him.

Franzi popped out like a terrified jack-in-the-box and immediately went behind Tabby, clinging to her legs like a hobble.

"Get in and go," Tabby told Clancy. "Before I change my mind."

Clancy opened his mouth, like he was considering some kind of final parting speech, then closed it. "Good-bye, cousin," he said instead. "You deserve her."

Logan snorted and snapped his teeth.

Tabby couldn't move, because of Franzi's death grip on her knees, so she was uncomfortably close to the car and unable to step back as it swung around in the wide drive and spat gravel behind it as it left. Logan trotted after it, presumably to make sure Clancy truly left, and Tabby lowered the gun in shaking hands as her knees finally gave out. She sank down to sit in the middle of the dark drive between the suitcases and drew Franzi into her lap.

Franzi had stopped shaking by the time Logan returned, and Tabby had plenty of time to second guess her decision to let Clancy go. What if he came back with goons? Was she always going to be afraid to go to sleep?

Should she have *shot* him? Tabby balked at even considering the option. What else could she *do*?

She gritted her teeth and rose up to greet Logan. Franzi was heavy, but no heavier than a bag of feed, and Tabby appreciated her desire to cling. How was she going to keep the little girl, when her legal guardian was a *horse*? "Did you lock the gate?" It had a pull-shut mechanism with a keypad; Logan should have been able to maneuver it shut if Clancy hadn't broken it on his way in. He'd probably had a keypad cracker like Logan did.

Logan nodded emphatically, and then snuffled her and Franzi thoroughly, making the little girl giggle and turn her face into Tabby's shoulder. "Let's have a glass of milk and go back to bed," she suggested.

Franzi nodded, but as Tabby started to walk back to the house, she suddenly went stiff.

Still on a hair-trigger, Tabby felt a stab of panic.

"My suitcases?" Franzi said quietly near her ear.

Tabby had to put her down to carry them in, and she found the gun she'd dropped with her foot. She shouldn't just leave it in the driveway, but she didn't want to take it inside with her. She lowered the suitcases to pick it up and shoved it down in the back of her truck under a shovel strapped in with a toolbox.

Franzi waited with the suitcases, Logan hovering behind her lipping her hair, and Tabby gave him a kiss on his big velvet-soft nose before she picked them back up and went into the house.

It was weirdly cheerful inside, well-lit and cozy after the cool night air. Tabby went to the fridge to get milk and saw her phone on the counter. Should she call someone? The cops were right out, and she wasn't sure it was worth waking Cherry in the middle of the night. What could her secret shifter agency do *now*?

She bumped the phone as she put out glasses, and stared at the notification on the screen. "Your Luggage, *Tabby's Tack*, has left its verified location."

There *was* something else she could do.

39

*T*abby wondered if the sounds of cars coming up her driveway would always bring back her feelings of terror and helplessness in the wake of Clancy's home invasion. "Stay here," she told Franzi firmly the next morning. "I'll see who it is."

The sight of a strange blue SUV that spilled out strange people wasn't very comforting. It looked more like a minivan than a government vehicle. "How did you get past the gate?"

"Aiden picked the lock," A dark-haired woman explained. "It's a really basic system. I'm Juliette. This is Aiden, and Noah is the suit." Aiden was wiry, wearing glasses, and grinning unrepentantly. Noah looked like he was wearing enough fabric for *two* suits, perfectly tailored for his rather beastly brawn.

"You could have texted first," Tabby said sharply. "Warning would have been nice."

"We weren't sure if Clancy would return, and we wanted to surprise him if he'd holed up here and was monitoring your phone," Juliette said calmly. "It looks like he didn't."

Was she so sure he wasn't because shifters could sense each other? Tabby still wasn't sure how far the ability extended. She felt like the magical one out and eyed the others curiously, wondering what their animals were. The big guy was probably a gorilla.

"We've got some paperwork to get started," Juliette said briskly. "I'd like to hear the entire story from the top. All the details you can remember. Can my guys look around the farm while we talk?"

"Sure," Tabby said faintly. "Oh, do you want his gun?"

Noah took it from her and wrapped it with surprising delicacy in a silk handkerchief from one of his pockets.

Tabby gave Juliette the tracking for the luggage tag. She'd slept with her phone, obsessively checking to make sure that the little blip on the map was comfortably far away. Clancy had driven about a hundred miles south and had stopped moving somewhere north of Butte. Tabby couldn't discount the idea that he'd found the tag and tossed it out, but she thought there was a real possibility it would never occur to him to look for it.

"This is all incredibly useful," Juliette said, after Tabby had talked herself hoarse and told her stories all out of order again. Juliette was a good listener, with excellent attention to detail, and she took Franzi's frequent interruptions in stride. She didn't seem to care that Tabby and Logan had competed in shows, though she was intrigued that there were other shifters in the classes, too. She frowned over the sale to Tallier, but didn't indicate that it would be problematic for Logan and Tabby. "We've got enough of a case to nail Clancy even without his crimes on file, and attempting to kidnap a shifter kid makes this a high priority. I'll get a team out there to bring him in and let you know when we've got him in custody."

"I'd like that," Tabby said with a sigh, as they went out to the porch. "It's been a lot."

Juliette's two guys were standing with Logan in the driveway and one of them had brought the felt board and letters out. They were clearly trying to communicate. Logan was miming something with his feet and face, twisting, to point his nose at his flank. Noah and Aiden were quizzing him, and Logan stamped in frustration.

"Can you do anything about Logan?"

"I'll get my team to investigate that," Juliette said. "It's not something we've ever run into."

Before they could get in earshot of her men, Tabby caught her arm. "What about Franzi?"

"We'll make sure Clancy is safely in custody," Juliette said.

"No, I mean about *her* custody. Logan is a *horse*."

"Her legal guardian is here on site," Juliette said with a shrug. "Our agency recognizes shifter autonomy in either form."

"I'm not sure that CPS will see it that way," Tabby reminded her. "What with that whole *not knowing about shifters* thing."

"We've got contacts in other departments," Juliette promised. "We won't let them take Franzi away from you."

Tabby felt like an iron band had been released from her heart. Someone was on their side. Someone, from the looks of it, with power and organization.

Aiden had a tablet out, and Logan was squinting at a map. He nosed around on the display, snorting when it didn't do what he wanted, and then pointed at an area and shook his head.

"My language skills in charade are a little rusty," Aiden

explained. "But, it seems like Logan got away with the branding iron that did this, and had to drop it on his way home. I want to try to find it! It could be the key to undoing Logan's little transformation problem here."

Logan nodded enthusiastically and pawed the ground.

"Let's mop up Clancy first," Juliette said briskly. "Before he changes his identity and moves out of our jurisdiction."

"What *is* your jurisdiction?" Tabby wanted to know.

Juliette winked at her. "That's classified."

Tabby was so relieved that she wasn't even annoyed, and she stood on the porch with Franzi as they drove away.

40

The only fly in the ointment of a perfect, blue-skied Labor Day was that Logan was still a horse, and no one had any idea how to turn him back.

Juliette's secret agency reported that they had captured Clancy, though they were vague about what they intended to *do* with him. They hadn't given up the hunt for the branding iron that Logan had left in the ditch in some vague hope that they could reverse-engineer what had happened to him, but Logan could tell that they weren't very optimistic about the prospect, and they had no other ideas for turning him back into a human.

Tabby and Franzi both swore that they liked him just as well as a horse, but Logan knew that he was a burden, and he despaired of ever being able to tuck Franzi into bed or pick her up when she fell. He couldn't drive her to day care, or go to his job and earn even a token paycheck. He couldn't even hang around the barn too obviously with Tabby, since he was still keeping a low profile as a horse and maintaining the fiction that he'd been sold.

And he couldn't make love to Tabby.

He missed the way his body felt with hers, limbs and skin together. She still kissed him, but it was a woman kissing her favorite horse. Tabby had him take horses out for exercise, using a long lead to guide them along the trails, but it felt like made-up work and Logan knew she was humoring his need to be useful.

Riding with her was both wonderful and deeply frustrating, especially when Tabby went bareback. She was so close...and so painfully far away. Logan was desperate to tell her all the feelings he was ready to admit, and had no way to do it or show it.

If it weren't for the companion in his head, Logan thought he'd have gone quietly mad.

Well, one of us has to have common sense, his stallion sniffed. *Stop wallowing in self-pity and enjoy the sunshine.*

"Is Tara here? Is Tara here?" Franzi was standing up on the bottom porch railing like she'd be able to see around the curve in the driveway if she was six inches taller.

"Her mom texted to let me know they were running a little late and that Dr. Becket was going to bring her," Tabby said patiently.

"Is the gate open? Can they get in?" Franzi wanted to know.

"I told them the combination," Tabby assured her.

The playset had been sanded and given a fresh coat of paint the day before, and it gleamed in the sun. Logan was doing the only gardening he really could nearby, munching chickweed carefully from around the vegetables.

He pricked his ears up suddenly just as Franzi shrieked, "They're here!" She jumped back off the porch railing so enthusiastically she ended up on her butt and bounced up without complaining. "Tara!"

"Don't run out in the driveway!" Tabby cautioned.

Logan heard the vehicle down the drive come forward and then pause as they must be closing the gate. That would be points in their favor with Tabby.

Franzi stood at the bottom of the porch, bouncing in place.

Logan melted back around the side of the house, then returned as Vivian's familiar car came into view.

A dark-haired man in scrubs got out of the driver's seat and extricated Tara, who hid behind him briefly as Tabby came forward to say hello. Franzi dashed forward and dragged Tara with her to the playset. "We're going to make TEA," she said commandingly. "You can make MUD!"

Logan lingered by the garden. As a man, he'd go forward and make conversation with Becket, commiserate about kids, and put his hand in Tabby's back pocket or around her waist to make sure that his claim on her was obvious.

But as a horse?

Should he butt in? Stay back? He was just livestock now, and maybe forever.

And you accuse **me** *of being dramatic*, his stallion huffed. *Go to him.* **Now.**

Logan noticed the little tingle of instinct just as his stallion spoke, and he sighed and walked forward.

"You must be Logan."

Logan gave a fancy half bow, folding one knee and arching his neck.

A little ostentatious, Logan's stallion sniffed.

You're always doing that kind of crap!

I do it better.

"Can I get you something to drink before you go?" Tabby offered.

But Becket was looking at Logan with his face a little

scrunched up in confusion. "There's something wrong with you."

*You **think?***

Logan's stallion was outraged. *There is nothing wrong with me. I am **perfect.***

It took Logan a moment to identify the feeling rising up in his throat as hope. *No, but there's something wrong with me. You said so yourself.*

*Oh. Yes, I suppose you are right. As long as we all realize there is nothing wrong with **me.***

"I heard about your predicament," Becket said, stretching out his hand but not offering to touch Logan until Logan stepped into it. "I wonder if I couldn't…help you fix it."

Tabby made a little not-daring-to-hope noise that Logan recognized from his own chest. "We've tried everything we could think of," she said softly. "What do you think you could do?"

Becket looked appraisingly at Tabby, frowning. "I'm not an ordinary shifter."

We're not an ordinary shifter, either, Logan's stallion snorted, not impressed by Becket's statement.

"I know that Tara is a kirin," Tabby said cautiously.

"Tara's not my daughter by blood," Becket said just as carefully. "But I'm a unicorn, too."

"I'm not sure what that means," Tabby admitted.

"I might be able to heal him. Magically."

Tabby sucked her breath in, and for a moment, the only sounds were the hum of the flies and Franzi's shrill directions to Tara in stirring mud for pies.

"That would be amazing," Tabby said, sounding choked. "What would I have to do?"

Becket licked his lips and returned his gaze to Logan, stroking his neck the way no one could help doing.

We are very strokable.

Becket walked down the length of Logan and peered at the brand on his flank before turning back to Tabby. "I'm going to shift, because it's a little easier for me, and I won't be able to speak while I work. You don't need to do anything but keep him still."

As if I was merely a farm animal! Logan's horse snorted.

Tabby nodded and went around the other side of Logan, keeping a hand on his nose.

Becket stepped back from Logan. "It won't look like anything is happening," he said, "but it's best if you don't disturb me." He glanced at the children, who were very happily engaged in their play.

Then he shivered in place, and was a unicorn.

He wasn't the same iridescent brown as Tara's Chinese unicorn, and he didn't have her scales, mane, or tiny antlers. He was a couple of hands shorter than Logan, but of the same general horse shape and grace. He was also pure white and had a pearly horn jutting from his forehead.

Totally over the top, Logan's stallion said with a mental eye roll, but Logan could tell he was jealous.

You're special, too, Logan assured him. *There's no one else in the world like you.*

The horse still pouted, but then Becket stepped forward and laid his gleaming horn on Logan's haunch where the brand marred his hide.

Becket's magic was not particularly comfortable as it flowed from the point of his horn.

It felt, for a moment, like Logan's skin was being turned inside out, or like he was getting an electric shock. It didn't hurt, exactly, but it was definitely unsettling. Tabby's hand on his head was like an anchor, and he had a moment of wondering if she felt it, too, like an electric current that went right through them.

Logan was aware of the scarred flesh burning away with a flash of discomfort into a new wound before it closed, sealing over where the brand had been with clean, undamaged hide. Even the hair grew back, prickling in its intensity.

Becket stepped back and shifted seamlessly into a man. "Did it work?"

For a moment, Logan was sure it hadn't. He was never going to be a person again. He didn't remember how. Then he went to bow his head in defeat, and his hat fell off at his feet.

He was back in his own skin, on his own legs, in clothing and boots, and tears of confusion and relief were tracing his cheeks.

"Logan!"

Tabby crashed into him and Logan finally had arms again to hold her close, and lips to kiss her, and that was all he could do for several minutes until Becket was backing away in embarrassment.

"I can, ah, just go say goodbye to Tara…"

Logan let Tabby go to arm's length and thrust a hand at Becket. "Thank you," he said gruffly, and it was so strange and wonderful to be able to speak that he said it again, "Thank you!" and then repeated it until the words had no meaning, continuing to shake Becket's hand until the poor man took it forcibly back.

"It's fine," Becket insisted, though he looked a little winded. "I'm happy I could help."

"Franzi!" Logan said, and it was the only thing that could have made him let go of Tabby as he dashed around the corner of the house to where the girls were still playing. "Franzi!"

Franzi, completely unfazed by his transformation, only waved. "I'm making tea, Uncle Logan! Come drink some!" All of her plastic dishes were spread out in the little play set, and Tara was putting mud food on little plates. Neither of them seemed to recognize that anything out of the ordinary had happened.

Franzi gave a little squeak of protest when Logan waded into their play to pick her up and crush her close. "You're winkling my dress, Uncle Logan," she chided. But she hugged back, her precious little arms tight around Logan's neck. "I missed you, too," she said solemnly. "Your tea is hot. Blow on it!"

Logan was deliriously happy to blow on his puddle-water tea and pretend to drink it, marveling on how his fingers worked and how balance worked on just two legs. He felt very small, powerless, and incredibly dextrous.

"I can't thank you enough," Tabby was saying, shaking Becket's hand almost as earnestly as Logan had. "Knowing that it had something to do with the brand didn't mean we could *do* anything about it."

"I'm just really glad it worked," Becket said kindly.

"Do you want to come in for some iced tea?" Tabby offered.

Logan literally salivated. Iced tea. *Real food.*

What's wrong with hay? his stallion wanted to know. **Nothing** *is better than alfalfa.*

Logan remembered again that he could speak out loud, but for the life of him, he couldn't think of a thing to say.

41

"How can I ever repay you?" Tabby asked Becket, trying to convince her eyes not to water.

Logan looked completely undone and was clearly trying to draw himself together, but Tabby didn't want to stop watching him, sure that he would vanish if she let him leave her sight.

Franzi and Tara looked singularly unimpressed and were already back at their play, but Tabby still felt as giddy as if she'd just been pushed off a cliff and realized she could fly.

"It's fine," Becket assured her, though he looked like he'd just finished a marathon. "No thanks necessary. I need to get to the clinic, but either Vivian or I will be back at about five thirty."

"Can we have you over for dinner? Or take you out later? Or take Tara for a weekend? A month?" Tabby knew that she was babbling and made herself stop. "We're just so, so grateful."

"I'm really happy I could help," Becket assured her,

and Tabby let him leave before she embarrassed herself by sobbing on him.

Logan was sitting in the garden with the kids, accepting mud pies and tea with weeds floating in it, and Tabby stood at the corner of the house and watched them, drinking the sight of him far more truly than he was drinking his questionable tea.

She had been slightly worried that she had imagined him too handsome in her head, that he could not possibly live up to her memory. Now that he was back, lean and gorgeous and wearing everything that he'd had on the last time she saw him, she realized that if anything, she'd underestimated the sheer beauty of his human form.

"Logan…"

Tabby hadn't meant to say his name out loud, only think it happily in her head, but it slipped from her lips. Logan looked over at once, and his face lit up with glee as he gave the girls excuses and sprang to his feet.

"Two legs!" he exclaimed, closing the distance between them to sweep her up into his arms.. "Two legs! Tabby, I *missed* you."

"You were right here," Tabby reminded him breathlessly, but she knew exactly what he meant. It had been a kind of sweet torture, having him so close and yet not there, not himself. She missed this—the hard press of his body and his hot kiss and his clever hands.

They sat together on the porch swing looking out over the garden and the playset, listening to Tara and Franzi playing, shamelessly cuddling because they couldn't do any more with their four-year-old chaperones.

"There has been so much I wanted to say," Logan said, laughing and nuzzling her hair. "And now that I can speak again, I just want to hold you and…" he whispered the rest in her ear, causing Tabby's cheeks to heat.

"Patience, stud," she chuckled. "It won't be that long until Tara goes home and Franzi goes to bed."

Logan groaned and had to adjust himself. "Would they even *notice* if we snuck off for about three minutes?"

"I am not settling for three minutes of you after waiting for over a month," Tabby chided him, but she stroked the inside of his thigh and pressed into his shoulder before turning to steal another kiss from him. "I *missed* you," she said honestly.

"I was right here," Logan echoed her as he kissed her, deeper and slower. "I was right here the whole time."

After they had kissed a little longer and Tabby's lips felt raw, he drew away. "I remember one of the things I wanted to say to you."

"Oh?" This wasn't the same kind of torment that not knowing when he would be human had been. He was hers again, and they just had to wait until after dinner and bedtime, and she'd have him for herself. It was a *when*, not an *if*.

"I love you," Logan said seriously, and the words were an electric thrill up Tabby's spine.

"I…l-love you," she said, stumbling over the words like she hadn't when he was a horse. "I *love* you."

"Marry me."

Tabby blinked at him and licked her lips. Her body was so on fire, and she was still more than a little in shock from seeing a perfectly normal doctor turn into a unicorn and heal her boyfriend, that she was beginning to feel a little like she was in a dream. Was dream-Logan asking her to marry her? Was she going to wake up to find that she'd never met him and was still trying to figure out how to make her mortgage payment?

"I probably should have done that better," Logan said, chagrined, because she was doing nothing more than staring at him, waiting for him to turn into a blaring alarm clock. "Will you accept the fact that I've been a horse for a month as an apology for being a clod?"

"You're not a clod," Tabby whispered.

"Then, will you marry me?" Logan begged. "I mean, I'm not against living in sin or whatever; sin is *super* fun. But I'd like Franzi to have a mom, and I'll probably have more luck adopting her if I've got a ring on your finger. And I don't want anyone else to ever have you. I want you to be mine forever, and I love you, Tabby. I love you *so much*."

"Why…?"

"I love your eyes and your hair and your ass," Logan said, touching each one in turn. "I love your indomitable spirit. I love that you were willing to do crimes with me, sort of, and that you took care of Franzi when I couldn't. I love how capable you are, and how you can fix all kinds of things, and how you ride and how you teach and how you cook, and the way you make me want to be a better person and that you show me how. I love how you're looking at me now, and how you never stop working and the way you fill up your shirt and how you twitch when you're sleeping."

Tabby had started laughing at some point and now wasn't sure how to stop. "I was going to ask you why it took you so long to ask me, Logan."

"Because I'm a fool," Logan said. "Because I spent the last month as a horse and I couldn't figure out how to get a ring."

"I don't need a ring," Tabby said honestly. "They just get in the way when I ride." She put a finger on Logan's mouth to cover his protest. "I fell in love with you the moment I set eyes on you and spent my life savings to buy you."

"Are you ever going to forgive me for that?" Logan asked, catching her hand to kiss it.

"Probably. When we're old and gray and have grandkids."

"Huh. I kind of love the idea of grandkids," Logan said. "And I bet you'll be really hot with silver hair."

"Uncle Logan?"

Tabby startled to find that Franzi and Tara had come up the stairs to the porch while Logan was proposing.

"We're hungry."

"You're filthy!" Tabby exclaimed. "How about a bath before lunch? Want me to hose you down like a horse?"

Both girls were very much in favor of this plan and Tara's parents had been wise enough to send a change of clothes and swimwear. Tabby had them switch into swimsuits and run through the sprinkler in the hot sun while she made lunch and laundered their clothes.

They ended the task almost muddier than before, but Tabby sacrificed two bath towels and got them mostly dry and clean enough to eat hot dogs and corn chips with cold lemonade sitting on the steps of the porch.

"Fu—" Logan glanced towards the girls. "—good grief. I have never tasted anything so amazing in my life." He ate his hot dog—and then a second one—like he hadn't had a square meal in a month. "Chips," he crowed, crunching them to the giggles of the girls. "CORN chips! Oh my god, NAPKINS!" He pretended to eat them.

Everything was absolutely wonderful.

After lunch, the girls quarreled briefly over how to play and settled on coloring in Franzi's 'horsey woom.'

"They're distracted," Logan said suggestively, raising an eyebrow at Tabby.

"Not distracted enough," Tabby said regretfully. "But

while you've got two hands, there *are* a few things I could use your help with."

Chores were much more fun with Logan there to reward her with hot kisses and whistle after her ass when she bent over to pick something up, and Tabby didn't even care that each one took twice as long.

Vivian arrived a few minutes late. "We had a fun rush of firecracker burns late in the afternoon," she said, as she peeled Tara away from Franzi. "We'll take you up on that offer for dinner later this week, I hope!"

Franzi was wound up and worn out from playing hard with Tara all day, and she was inclined to be defiant and pouty when she didn't get her way, but Logan deftly distracted her every time she was on the brink of a fit, and he spent the time that Tabby was making dinner playing in her room with her.

Predictably, the little girl popped right out of bed after she was put down, first to go potty, then to get a drink, then because she needed a hug. "No, not from Uncle Logan, from AUNT TABBY!" Tabby tucked her back in and she had a moment of hope after she closed the door when there was silence.

Then, "NOW I NEED A HUG FROM UNCLE LOGAN!"

Logan took a turn tucking her in. "Stay in bed, pumpkin," he begged. "It's time for sleeping."

"I'm not sleepy," Franzi insisted, her mouth deforming around a yawn.

"Try to sleep anyway," Logan suggested. "Close your eyes and think about pickles."

Franzi giggled. "Sing me the song!"

They sang the lullaby together, while Tabby fidgeted outside the door and wished that they would hurry *up*.

When Logan came out and shut the door, he pulled

her into her arms and kissed her, but they went to the living room instead of the bedroom, sure that this wasn't Franzi's final gambit.

"I didn't get an actual answer about marrying me," Logan said, as he kissed her neck.

"You don't have to marry me," Tabby said. They sat together on the couch stroking each other but not daring to undress because of the inevitable pending interruption.

Logan drew back. "Do you not want me to marry you?"

"No, I do!" Tabby was quick to assure him. "It's just that you've been a horse for a month and you're finally human. Probably this is one of those things that you shouldn't make big decisions after, like major surgery or grief. We could wait. You could ask me again in a week. But I'm serious about not bothering with a ring."

"I don't want to wait," Logan said, his voice—and oh, it was so wonderful to hear his voice!—low and full of feeling. "I love you, Tabby Swiftwater. I love you to your toes, and I want to be with you forever."

"I'll marry you." Tabby rose up in his arms and kissed him, and she wasn't sure how he got her shirt off, but it occurred to her some time later that there was still silence from Franzi's room, and it would be a lot more comfortable in the bedroom. "C'mon stud," she told Logan, pulling him up with her. "I'm going to get my money's worth."

EPILOGUE

*L*ogan wondered if he would always feel a little jealous when Tabby rode another horse.

The mare under her, Poppy, had been training over the fences all winter, and if she was comparatively short and less distinctly marked than Logan, she was still a pretty horse, and she listened to Tabby and jumped joyously.

The steps they did weren't nearly as theatrical as Logan's shows had been, but they were a solid team, and moved together well, nailing every jump.

Tabby and Poppy finished the final course with no faults and the mare gave a nicker of pleasure as the audience burst into applause and Tabby leaned forward to hug her neck and praise her.

They weren't as good as we were, his stallion sniffed, as the pair came out of the ring in triumph.

It was still an impressive show, and Tabby swung down out of the saddle straight into Logan's arms. "We did it," she said joyfully. "We did it!"

"I knew you would," Logan agreed, kissing her and

swinging her around in a circle for good measure. Poppy snorted and backed up a few unappreciative steps.

"I'd be happy with *any* ribbon," Tabby said. "I just really wanted to prove to myself that I had what it took, that it wasn't just *Beau* that won last time."

"I see how it is," Logan groaned. "Strip me of all my honor and glory. No, it's fine. Never mind my ego in the dust, here. I'm sure I needed some humility."

"You do," Tabby said without mercy. "Have you seen the way you've been strutting around lately?"

Logan thought he'd done a better job hiding his pride, but it seemed like everything was falling into place. His life was taking a shape for perfect happiness, in ways that he never would have guessed possible.

Mason had not only given him his job back when he was human again, but also moved him into an official mentorship, months before he was technically due for it.

Better than that, child services had authorized Logan's application to officially adopt Franzi.

And best of all...

There is the rest of our herd! his stallion trilled as Letisha came through the crowd with Franzi's hand held firmly in her own.

"Congratulations, Miss Swiftwater!" she said, releasing Franzi to run up to Logan and get swept up into the air.

"The bathroom here is a HUNDRED MILES!" Franzi exclaimed.

Logan wasn't sure if she was saying it was a hundred miles away or a hundred miles across inside. He guessed she hadn't seen many public restrooms. "Thanks for taking her," he told Letisha. "I didn't want to miss Tabby's big win."

"Thank you!" Tabby said, giving both girls a swift hug.

"And congratulations to you for getting qualified, Letisha! That's amazing progress! I'm so proud of you!"

Letisha blushed and grinned. "What an amazing show! I'm going to go find my mom!" she said enthusiastically. "See you next Saturday!"

"I guess that was a pretty good last ride," Logan told Tabby, lifting Franzi up to sit on his shoulders.

"Not the last ride *ever*," Tabby protested. "Just the last one for a few months."

"Six. Six months." Her belly already had a little soft swell to it, barely noticeable beneath her shirt, and Logan could not help smiling down at it. "It'll be worth it."

Our herd, his stallion crowed in delight.

"You're not the one who has to give up half a year of riding and pop a bowling ball out of your…"

"Ms. Swiftwater?"

Logan drew Franzi away to look at *more horsies* as Tabby accepted congratulations for her win and worked her persuasive magic on a potential client.

They wandered the aisles of the sprawling stable and Logan carried Franzi so she could see the horses over their doors and pet the heads that were offered.

"Uncle Logan?"

"Yeah, kitten?"

"When I'm a flower girl, will you be my dad?"

Logan had made several efforts to explain marriage and adoption to Franzi, but he wasn't sure how much of it she really understood.

"Do you want me to be your dad, Franzi?"

Franzi had a moment of thoughtful stillness that Logan would never have expected to find in a five-year old before he met her. Then she gave a slight wiggle that indicated she wanted down. Logan swung her back down to the ground and his shoulders gave a little ache of gratitude;

she was growing like a summer weed and he wouldn't be able to give her rides as a human for many more years.

"I like you, Uncle Logan," Franzi said with a firm nod. "You can be my dad. And Tabby can be my mom and Tara can be my sister."

"You're going to have your own brother or sister," Logan reminded her.

"I don't want a baby. I want Tara to be my sister."

"I don't think that we can just trade kids," Logan said in despair. Then he wondered if Franzi was secretly worried that they would trade her away. He crouched down so he could look her in the eyes. "I love you, Franzi-pants. I love you to the moon and back. I won't ever give you away. I'll love your brother or sister, too, but not more than you. Just the same. You'll both be my kids and I wouldn't trade you ever. Not even for chocolate."

Franzi frowned suspiciously. "What about TOFFEE chocolate."

"Oh," Logan pretended to think. "I might trade you for toffee chocolate."

Franzi's eyes got big, but she grinned and Logan was glad that she seemed to know he was joking. "Nope. Not going to trade you, even for TOFFEE chocolate. Let's go find Tabby and we can trade HER for toffee chocolate."

"Nooooooo!" Franzi wailed, completely along for the ride now. "Tabby has to be my MOMMY."

"Maybe we can turn her INTO toffee chocolate, and then EAT her," Logan suggested. "Yum, yum, yum…"

They pelted back to find that Tabby had bedded Poppy down and collected a fistful of business cards that she flashed at Logan triumphantly. "We're here to eat you," Logan announced, drawing her close and nibbling on her neck.

"Not in front of the children, darling," Tabby demurred.

"Well, Franzi won't let me trade you for toffee chocolate," Logan pouted. "She says you have to be her mom."

Tabby looked down at Franzi with a melting smile. "Aw, Franzi, that's the sweetest. What do you have on your face?"

Logan bent to wipe the mysterious mess from Franzi's face with the back of his sleeve. "Let's go pack up, Mrs. Swiftwater-Kennedy."

"I'm not doing a hyphen," Tabby scolded him, but she smiled. "You could always be *Mr.* Swiftwater."

"You know, we don't have to limit ourselves to patriarchal traditions. We could pick any names we like. I know a guy in Detroit who can make us new documents for any identity we want."

"That guy folded like a wet paper towel when I sent my investigator after him," Tabby reminded him.

"So I'll probably get a really good deal on it," Logan teased. "Who do you want to be? Mrs. Rockefeller? Mrs. Monroe? You could change your first name, too."

"I'm not going to be Marilyn Monroe," Tabby laughed. "We're both taking Franzi's name. I'm going to be Mrs. *Kennedy*. Your wife. Your *one.*"

Logan had to catch her up for a kiss for that, of course. "I love you, Tabby Whateveryourlastnameis. I love you forever."

"I'm bored," Franzi complained. "Can we go?"

Herd, his stallion nickered happily. *Our mate, our filly, and our foal. Forever.*

A NOTE FROM ELVA

This book was a runaway at times, and I am particularly grateful for my early readers who yanked on the reins when I made glaring horse faux pas (and there were many!). Any errors that remain are solely my own. I hope you love Franzi and Logan and Tabby as much as I loved writing them. I'm looking forward to returning to Nickel City in Raven's Instinct and am already compiling notes! Will we find out some of Cherry's secrets? What happens when Amy tries to fly?

Questions? Suggestions? Did you find typos? Want to send fan mail? Email me at elvaherself@elvabirch.com!

I always appreciate your reviews and read them all!

~Elva

Want some more extra short stories? Join my mailing list for sneak previews, extras, bonus stories, and more, or join my Reader's Retreat on Facebook!

A Day Care for Shifters: A feel-good series about adorable shifter kids and their struggling single parents in a town full of mystery and surprise. Start the series with

Wolf's Instinct, when Addison comes to Nickel City to take a job at a very special day care and finds a family to belong to. A gentle ice-cream-straight-from-the-container escape. Sweet and sizzling!

The Royal Dragons of Alaska: A fascinating alternate world where Alaska is ruled by secret dragon shifters. Adventure, romance, and humor! Reluctant royalty, relentless enemies…dogs, camping, and magic! Start with The Dragon Prince of Alaska.

Suddenly Shifters: A hilarious series of novellas, serials, and shorts set in the small town of Anders Canyon, where something (in the water?) is making ordinary citizens turn into shifters. Start with Something in the Water!

Lawn Ornament Shifters: The series that was only supposed to be a joke, this is a collection of short, ridiculous romances featuring unusual shifters, myths, and magic. Cross-your-legs funny and full of heart! Start with The Flamingo's Fated Mate!

Birch Hearts: An enchanting collection of short stories and novellas. Unconstrained by theme or setting, each short read has romance, magic, and heart, with a satisfying conclusion. And always, the impossible and irresistible. Start with a sampler plate in Prompted 2 for fourteen pieces of sweet-to-sizzling flash fiction, or dive in with the novella, Better Half - which you can get free for joining my mailing list at elvabirch.com!

peril and steamy! Standalone books where you can revisit your favorite characters - this series is also complete with six books! Start with Dancing Bearfoot! This series crosses over with **Virtue Shifters**, which starts with Timber Wolf.

BEHIND THE SCENES

What is Patreon?

Patreon is a site where readers and fans can support creators with monthly subscriptions.

At my Patreon, I have tiers with early rough drafts of my books, flash fiction, coloring pages, signed and sketched paperbacks, exclusive swag, original artwork, photographs…and so much more! Every month is a little different, and there is a price for every budget. Patreon allows me to do projects that aren't very commercial and makes my income stream a little less unpredictable. It also gives me a place to connect with my fans!

Come find out what's going on behind the scenes and keep me creating at Patreon! patreon.com/ellenmillion

Carina Andresen surged to her feet, sweeping her camp chair out from under her as a make-shift weapon.

Wolf! her brain hammered at her. *Wolf!* She was going to become an Alaska tourist statistic and get eaten by a wolf on her second week in the kingdom.

Logic slowly caught up with her panic.

The animal across the campfire from her was smaller and *doggier* than a wolf, and it was only a moment before Carina could get her breath and heartbeat back under control and recognize that it was well-groomed, shyly eyeing her sizzling hot dog, and wagging its tail.

Alaska probably had stray dogs, too; she wasn't *that* far from civilization.

"Hi there, sweetie," Carina said, her voice still unnaturally high as she put her chair back on its legs. "Does that smell good? Want a bit of hot dog?" Carina turned the hot dog in the flame and waggled it suggestively.

The non-edible dog sped up his tail and when Carina broke off a piece of the meat and dropped it beside her, he crept around the fire and slurped it eagerly up off the ground.

The second bite he took gently from her fingers, and by the second hot dog she dared to pet him.

Within about thirty minutes and five hot dogs, he was leaning on her and letting her scratch his ears and neck as he wagged his tail and groaned in delight.

"Oh, you're just a dear," Carina said. "I bet someone's missing you." He was a husky mix, Carina guessed; he was tall and strong, with a long, thick coat of dark gray fur and white feet. His ears were upright, and his tail was long and feathered. He didn't have a collar, but he was clearly friendly. "You want some water?"

The dog licked his lips as if he had understood, and Carina carefully stood so she didn't frighten him.

But he seemed to be past any shyness now, and he followed Carina to her van trustingly, tail waving happily. He drank the offered water from a frying pan, and then tried to give Carina a kiss dripping with slobber.

"You probably already have a name," Carina said, laughingly trying to escape the wet tongue. "But I'm going to call you Shadow for now." She had a grubby towel hanging from her clothesline and used it to dry off his face.

They played a gentle game of tug-of-war, testing each other's strength and manners.

Shadow seemed to approve of his new name and gave her a canine grin once she'd won the towel back from him.

"Alright, Shadow, let's go collect some more firewood."

The area was rich with downed wood to harvest, and with the assistance of a folding hand saw, Carina was able to find several heaping armloads of solid, dry wood, enough to keep a cheerful fire going for a few days if she was frugal. It was comforting to have Shadow around for the task; she wasn't quite as nervous about the noises she heard, and he was a happy distraction from her own brain.

He frolicked with her, and found a stick three times his own length to drag around possessively.

"So helpful!" Carina laughed at him, as he knocked over an empty pot and swiped her across the knees so that she nearly fell.

When she sat down beside the crackling fire in her low camp chair, Shadow abandoned his prize stick and crowded close to lay his head on her knee. Carina petted him absently.

"Someone's looking for you, you big softy," she said regretfully. She would have to try to reunite the dog with his owner but, for now, it was nice having a companion around the camp.

Of all the things she expected when she went running for the wilderness, she had never guessed that the silence would be the worst. She had been camping plenty, but it was always *with* someone. Since their parents had died, that someone was usually her sister, June, but sometimes it was a friend or a roommate. She was used to having someone to point out birds and animals to, someone to share chores with, stretch out tarps with. When it was just her, the spaces seemed vaster, the wind bit harder, and even the birds were less cheerful.

"You probably don't care about the birds that would make my life list," she told Shadow mournfully.

Shadow wagged his tail in a rustle of leaves.

She didn't have her life list anymore to add to anyway. Everything had been left behind: her phone, her computer, her identity. Her entire life was on hold. She had the van to live in, some supplies and a small nest egg to start from, so she ought to be able to stay out of sight long enough to regroup and…she didn't know what to do from here. Find a journalist willing to take her story and clear her name?

To fill the quiet, and to help ignore the ache in her chest, she read aloud from the brochure on Alaska that she had been given at the border station. She'd found it that evening while she was emptying the glovebox to take stock of supplies, and Shadow seemed as good a listener as any.

"Like many modern monarchies, Alaska has an elected council of officials who do most of the day to day rulings of this vast, rich land. The royal family is steeped in tradition and mystery, and holds many veto powers, as well as acting as ambassadors to other countries. Known as the Dragon King, the Alaskan sovereign is a reserved figure who rarely appears in public. Margaret, the Queen of Alaska, died twelve years ago, leaving behind six sons." There was a photo, with boys ranging from about seven to maybe twenty-five. Two of the middle children were identical. One of the twins was wearing a hockey jersey and grinning, the other wore glasses and looked annoyed. The oldest—or at least the tallest—was frowning seriously at the others. The only blonde of the bunch was one of the middle boys, who was looking intently at the camera. The youngest looked painfully bored. They all had tongue-twisting names of more syllables than Carina wanted to try pronouncing.

Carina thought it was an interesting photo. The tension between the oldest two was palpable, and the they were all dressed surprisingly casually. She didn't follow royal gossip much beyond scanning headlines at grocery store checkouts, but Alaska never seemed to make waves; they were rarely involved in dramas and scandals.

Shadow raised his head and cocked his head at some imagined noise in the forest.

"That's a lot of siblings," Carina observed, ruffling his ears. She felt so much safer having him beside her. "Just one sister was more than enough for me." She didn't want to admit how much she missed that sister right now.

Shadow returned his head to her knee. "Alaska is a member of the Small Kingdoms Alliance, an exclusive collective of independent monarchies scattered throughout the world."

Carina turned the brochure over. "There are hot springs about fifty miles north of Fairbanks! I hope to make it there." *Before* she ran out of cash. It looked expensive. Maybe she could get work there...she'd heard that it wasn't hard to find under-the-table jobs in this country.

Shadow suddenly leapt to his feet, barking at something crashing through the woods behind them and Carina nearly tipped over backwards in her camp chair trying to stand up.

She expected to find a moose, or possibly a bear, and she was already picking up the chair to use as a flimsy defense against a charging wild animal.

But it was only a man stepping out of the woods, in an official dark blue uniform emblazoned with the eight gold stars of Alaska.

For a moment, terror every bit as keen as the panic that

had gripped her at the first sight of Shadow washed over her. They'd found her.

"You're trespassing on royal land and I'm going to have to ask you to leave," he said.

Then she realized with relief that it wasn't a police officer. He was only a park ranger.

…or was he? Discover love and adventure in a wonderful alternate Alaska with camping and dogs and magic, reluctant royalty and relentless enemies! Pick up The Dragon Prince of Alaska *today!*